Angela Thirkell

Angela Thirkell, granddaughter ...d Burne-Jones, was born in London in 1890. At the age of twenty-eight she moved to Melbourne, Australia where she became involved in broadcasting and was a frequent contributor to British periodicals. Mrs. Thirkell did not begin writing novels until her return to Britain in 1930; then, for the rest of her life, she produced a new book almost every year. Her stylish prose and deft portrayal of the human comedy in the imaginary county of Barsetshire have amused readers for decades. She died in 1961, just before her seventy-first birthday.

"*Coronation Summer,* first published in England in [the 1930's] charmingly shows us Queen Victoria's coronation through the eyes of Fanny Harcourt, a delightfully unsophisticated Victorian woman who has just enough malicious insight to make her view of people and events interesting."

— *Saturday Review*

"Vintage Thirkell, and a new generation of readers will now enjoy it."

— *Times* [London] *Literary Review*

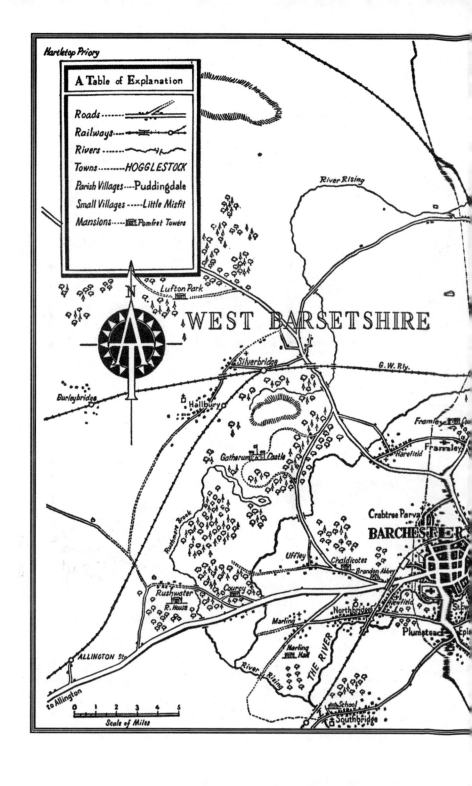

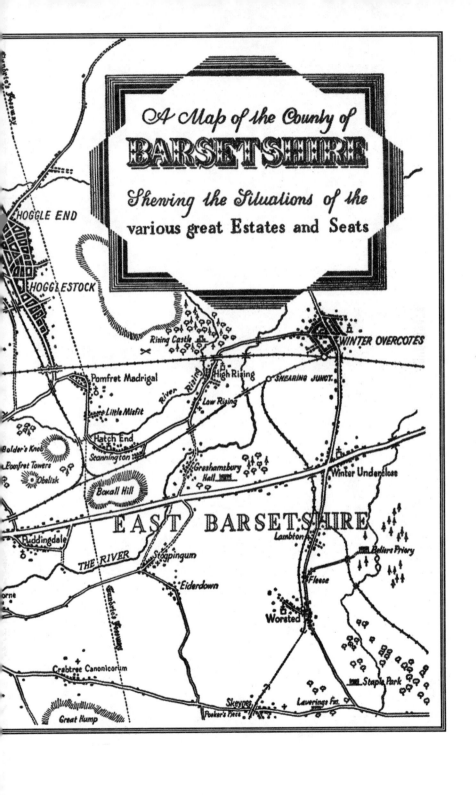

Contents

*I*N 1840 the Reverend Richard Barham brought out the first series of Ingoldsby Legends, pretending that they were the work of a Thomas Ingoldsby, Esquire. Mrs. Thirkell has invented a young married woman, the neighbour of a genuine Mr. Thomas Ingoldsby; and this young lady's mystified reading, upon its first publication, of the supposed work of her acquaintance, including Mr. Barney Maguire's Account of the Coronation of Queen Victoria, recalls to her mind her own visit to London for the Coronation festivities. And so in this book we have London (and Epsom, and Eton) as they were when his present Majesty's great-grandmother was crowned.

ILLUSTRATIONS

*Acknowledgments are due in each case to the owner whose name appears
below, and in particular to Her Majesty the Queen for gracious permission
to reproduce Sir David Wilkie's "Queen Victoria holding her first Council"
from the Windsor Castle Collection.*

CHAPTER I

AT TAPTON HALL

Tapton Hall, Kent.
1840

A few mornings ago a large parcel of books and papers came from town for my husband. As Mr. Darnley likes to open his own parcels, I waited till he was engaged with his bailiff and then rang the bell. When the footman answered it, I requested him to take the packet into the library, where I knew Mr. Darnley would not be likely to make his appearance till nearly dinner-time. As soon as I was alone I eagerly opened the parcel, taking care, however, to do so in such a way that I could do it up again without Mr. Darnley being any the wiser. This is indeed not hypocrisy on my part, but I find that the wheels of life often run far more smoothly if well greased, and Mr. Darnley, though the best of husbands, does not always control his temper over trifles. In this respect he is not unlike my dear Papa, whose ebullitions of temper were so trying to my dear Mamma, and indeed to his whole family, that it is a matter for self-gratulation that Mr. Darnley's house at Tapton is well out of Papa's reach. Papa has often most solemnly asseverated, indeed with a use of language which dear Mamma used to consider quite unjustifiable, that he will never set foot in one of those new-fangled railway coaches. But as there is little fear of the railway mania spreading into his dear Norfolk, nor indeed into our rural

Kent—or so I thought till lately—it is unlikely that the temptation will assail him, and considering his years and his gout, together with his at present far from affluent condition, it is hardly probable that he will make the journey by coach. So we may consider ourselves fairly safe from a visit which, welcome though it would be, could hardly fail to be otherwise than productive of the greatest annoyance and inconvenience both to myself and Mr. Darnley. Papa has not yet seen his first grandchild, my and Mr. Darnley's dear little Victoria, for my excellent nurse, Mrs. Baker, does not wish to undertake so fatiguing a journey at her age. Willingly would I go myself and put up with Papa's ways for a month or so in the cause of filial duty, for he is low in his spirits since Mamma died, but that an event is expected within the next six months which, while adding to the number of the inmates of Tapton Hall, will also put travelling out of the question for me for some time to come. But I have said enough.

Hardly had I released the books from their wrapping when a knock at the door startled me. Controlling my emotions, for the sake of one who shall be nameless, I cried out, "Come in," at the same time placing myself before the table on which the half-opened parcel lay, so that the newcomer should not immediately perceive what I had been doing. But on the footman's announcing Miss Dacre, all my fears fled. It was indeed Emily Dacre, my dearest friend, and one who will shortly I hope be a sister to me, as will appear later in this narration. Her father is the rector of this village, and as his demise may be confidently though regretfully expected at an early date, the third stroke being almost invariably fatal, and the living is in Mr. Darnley's gift, that most indulgent of husbands has promised it to my dear elder brother Ned, who will then lead Emily as a bride to the home which she has so long adorned as a daughter. This, though convenient, will lack the charm of novelty, but as Emily is quite devoted to Ned, she will doubtless find novelty in seeing his handsome head with its black curls upon the conjugal pillow, though I confess that to me the thought of sharing with my husband the room formerly occupied by my parents would have in it something embarrassing, though I do not observe that Mr. Darnley, not being of my sensitive disposition, has felt any similar qualms in the case of our own establishment. But then his parents have been dead for many years, his mother in fact having lost her life in giving life to him, and his father and he having been on very bad terms until old Mr. Darnley luckily died some ten years ago, leaving my Henry the heir to his considerable fortune. The palliasses at the rectory will, of course, be entirely re-made, and Ned is determined to change the position of the bed from its present place near the door to the opposite end of the room, so that he may be able to see the stables, so Emily, whose feelings are not so painfully sensitive as mine, will probably not sustain the shock to her finer feelings which I should experience in a similar case.

Emily, looking blooming in her morning dress and chip bonnet, entered the room.

"What are you doing, my dear creature?" was her first question.

"Undoing this packet of books and papers from town," I replied.

"I thought," cried Emily, "that Mr. Darnley did not wish his parcels to be opened by any hand but his own. But let me see, dearest Fanny, what the bookseller has sent."

Throwing her bonnet and shawl onto a chair, Emily officiously assisted me to look through the contents of the package.

"Heavens! what a horrid set!" she exclaimed. "Nothing by our dear Boz! *Sordello*; what is that? Oh, poetry. Poetry is dead since dear Lord Byron died. *Ten Thousand a Year?* That must be of interest. That terrible *Weekly Despatch*! Ned will not hear of it. You remember how angry it made him when we were in London for the Coronation and you and I used to read it on the sly. Ned is delighted that that wicked Alderman Harmer is not to be Lord Mayor. Ned says that a man who owns such a subversive paper, who is so rude about our young Queen, is little more than an infidel. Ned will only read *The Times,* or the *Morning Post.* Now if only there were something by Bulwer, like his charming *Leila*—a doat of a book. Ned did not like it though. Ned says that he will not have any book by Bulwer in the Rectory, that they appeal to the passions. What else? *The Voyage of the Beagle? The Athenaeum?* My dear Fanny, how I pity you. Why does not Mr. Darnley get *The Old Curiosity Shop* by our dear Boz? Do you remember, Fanny, how we used to make Ned get us that wicked *Bell's Life* when we were in London, that we might see the pictures from *Oliver Twist* and *Pickwick* in the Gallery of Comicalities? Ned says that though Mr. Dickens is hardly a gentleman, he has done as much good as twenty of these rubbishing new Factory Inspectors or Police Commissions."

But I had had enough. Dear as Emily is to me, and dearer yet as she will be, there is something inexpressibly annoying in the way she rattles on about Ned, who is after all only to be the rector, and has not the knowledge of the world, nor the advanced opinions that Mr. Darnley possesses. Mr. Darnley is a man of the world, while Ned only lately came down from Cambridge. To change the subject I said with some coldness:

"Here is a book, Emily, which promises amusement mingled with instruction, whatever Ned's feelings may be about Mr. Dickens."

I held up a volume entitled *The Ingoldsby Legends,* by Thomas Ingoldsby.

"Old, my dear, old!" cried Emily in her provoking way. "I am sure I heard about them from Ned at least a year ago. They appeared in *Bentley's Miscellany.* Silly rubbish I am certain. Ned says——"

"Oh, spare me Ned," I cried, now thoroughly out of temper, "and let me tell you, dearest Emily, that Mr. Darnley does not subscribe to that magazine. Were it worth reading, doubtless he would do so."

"Well, Fanny," said Emily, "if Mr. Darnley does not approve of *Bentley's Miscellany,* doubtless he would not wish you to read the books that are extracted from it. So let me have *The Ingoldsby Legends*, and do you read *The Voyage of the Beagle*. Ned hopes to have a pack himself."

While thoroughly vexed with Emily, I could not but admit privately that I had put myself in the wrong by my hasty words about *Bentley's*, so composing myself upon the couch with *The Voyage of the Beagle*, I began to read. Science, my dear Papa has often said, though here he and Mr. Darnley are not in agreement, is no pursuit for a gentleman, and under the influence of Mr. Darwin's—whoever he may be—account of what appears to have been a long and monotonous voyage, I sank into a state of semi-unconsciousness, from which I was roused by Emily.

"Listen, Fanny," she cried, in a voice from which all traces of ill humour had now vanished, "this is most peculiar. You know the Ingoldsbys at Tappington Everard."

"Of course I know the Ingoldsbys," said I. "You know well, Emily, that you yourself introduced the whole family to me when we were in town for the Coronation; old Mr. Ingoldsby, Mr. Tom Ingoldsby, his son, and Mr. and Mrs. Charles Seaforth, his daughter and son-in-law, and that I am godmother to Mrs. Seaforth's third child. It seems to me to be very foolish to ask a question to which you already know the answer. What is in your mind?"

"I cannot understand it at all," was Emily's reply.

"Understand what, my love?" I asked with some acerbity, hating all mysteries.

"Why, that Tom Ingoldsby, Mrs. Seaforth's brother, should have written such a curious book. I have known the family ever since we came here, but this is not at all like them. All kinds of ghost stories, beginning with a highly diverting story about Charles Seaforth walking in his sleep without his breeches——"

"Emily!" I ejaculated.

"Can it really be Tom Ingoldsby, do you think? Or is it all a hoax?"

"How can I tell, Emily," said I, with all the dignity of a wife and mother, both present and prospective, "if you so selfishly keep to yourself the book, which after all is Mr. Darnley's property, and you know how he feels about any one reading his books before he has seen them himself. It is exactly the same with the post-bag. You had better hand the volume to me, Emily, so that I may judge for myself."

Here a regrettable incident occurred, the book somehow being wrenched between Emily and myself, with the unhappy result that a page was torn. Consternation stared us in the face. What would Mr. Darnley say was the question that rose unbidden to both our lips. Emily, who is of a bolder and less delicate nature than myself, was the first to speak.

"Fanny!" she cried, "Mr. Darnley must never see this book. Let us do up the parcel," said she, suiting the action to the word, "and you must hide *The Ingoldsby Legends* among your private possessions."

"You do not seem to understand, Emily," I retorted, "that a wife should have no secrets from her husband."

But as Emily only replied, "Stuff and nonsense," I resigned myself to a perusal of the book, the cause of the commotion. Suddenly I in my turn became convulsed with emotion.

"Emily!" I cried. "You are right."

"I always am," replied that provoking Emily.

"Not always, my dearest creature," said I, "but in this case you are. It is indeed a curious book. Listen to this."

I then read aloud, and Mr. Darnley has been pleased to say that I read with admirable taste, the following paragraph from the *Ingoldsby Legends:*

"It was in the summer of 1838 that a party from Tappington reached the metropolis with a view of witnessing the coronation of their youthful Queen, whom God long preserve!— This purpose they were fortunate enough to accomplish by the purchase of a peer's ticket, from a stationer in the Strand, who was enabled to dispose of some, greatly to the indignation of the hereditary Earl Marshal. How Mr. Barney managed to insinuate himself into the Abbey remains a mystery: his characteristic modesty and address doubtless assisted him, for there he unquestionably was. The result of his observations was thus communicated to his associates in the Servants' Hall upon his return, to the infinite delectation of *Mademoiselle Pauline* over a *Cruiskeen* of his own concocting."

"And then," I concluded, "there follows a poem."

Emily, as she tied the last knot in the parcel, turned to me a countenance whose expression showed the highest degree of interest and bewilderment.

"But, dearest Fanny," she cried, "what can this mean? This paragraph evidently refers to the visit of the Ingoldsby family to town for the Coronation—you know we met them there. But they have no servant called Barney. Charles Seaforth did indeed have an Irishman in his service called Thady or some such name, but the fellow could not have written poetry. I confess, Fanny, that I am completely bambaized."

Without commenting on this word, doubtless a piece of Ned's Cambridge slang, "I will, my dear," said I, "read aloud to you the poem which follows. We can then form some decision as to the nature of the work."

Accordingly I proceeded to read the effusion, though sorely tried by Emily's tiresome habit of interrupting.

"It is entitled," I began, "'Mr. Barney Maguire's Account of the Coronation.' It reads thus:"

Och! the Coronation! what celebration
    For emulation can with it compare?
When to Westminster the Royal Spinster,
    And the Duke of Leinster, all in order did repair!
'Twas there you'd see the New Polishemen
    Making a skrimmage at half after four,

> And the Lords and Ladies, and the Miss O'Gradys
>   All standing round before the Abbey door.
>
> Their pillows scorning, that self-same morning
>   Themselves adorning, all by the candle light,
> With roses and lilies, and daffy-down-dillies,
>   And gould, and jewels, and rich di'monds bright.
> And then approaches five hundred coaches,
>   With Giniral Dullbeak.—Och! 'twas mighty fine
> To see how asy bould Corporal Casey,
>   With his swoord drawn, prancing, made them kape
>   the line.

"We did indeed have to get up shockingly early," said Emily, but I read on.

> Then the Guns' alarums, and the King of Arums,
>   All in his Garters and his Clarence shoes,

"Pray, what does the creature mean by Clarence shoes?" asked Emily.

"Perhaps," said I with some coldness, "you have never heard of Clarenceux King of Arms. Would you prefer me to stop?"

"No, go on. It was doubtless the way you read it that made me mistake."

Without taking any notice of this I continued:

> Opening the massy doors to the bould Ambassydors,
>   The Prince of Potboys, and great haythen Jews;
> 'Twould have made you crazy to see Esterhazy
>   All jew'ls from jasey to his di'mond boots,
> With Alderman Harmer, and that swate charmer,
>   The female heiress, Miss Anjā-ly Coutts.

SIR DAVID WILKIE'S NOBLE PICTURE

LAYING THE WOOD PAVEMENT IN OXFORD STREET

And Wellington walking with his swoord drawn, talking
  To Hill and Hardinge, haroes of great fame;
And Sir De Lacy, and the Duke Dalmasey,
  (They call'd him Sowlt afore he changed his name,)
Themselves presading Lord Melbourne, lading
  The Queen, the darling, to her Royal chair,
And that fine ould fellow, the Duke of Pell-Mello,
  The Queen of Portingal's Chargy-de-fair.

"Well," I ejaculated, "what extraordinary blunders the fellow
does make. Pell-Mello for Palmella. Why, everyone in town
who was anybody knew Palmell."

"If you are tired, Fanny," said Emily, "I will willingly continue
the reading for you."

This was not to be borne. In a loudish voice and not heed-
ing any of Emily's attempts to interrupt, I went on with the
reading.

Then the Noble Prussians, likewise the Russians,
  In fine laced jackets with their goulden cuffs,
And the Bavarians, and the proud Hungarians,
  And Everythingarians all in furs and muffs.
Then Misthur Spaker, with Misthur Pays the Quaker,
  All in the Gallery you might persave,
But Lord Brougham was missing, and gone a fishing,
  Ounly crass Lord Essex would not give him lave.

There was Baron Alten himself exalting,
  And Prince Von Swartzenberg, and many more,
Och! I'd be bother'd, and entirely smother'd
  To tell the half of 'em was to the fore;
With the swate Peeresses, in their crowns and dresses,
  And Aldermanesses, and the Boord of Works;
But Mehemet Ali said, quite gintaly,
  "I'd be proud to see the likes among the Turks!"

Then the Queen, Heaven bless her! och! they did dress her
    In her purple garaments, and her goulden Crown;
Like Venus or Hebe, or the Queen of Sheby,
    With eight young Ladies houlding up her gown.
Sure 'twas grand to see her, also for to he-ar
    The big drums bating, and the trumpets blow,
And Sir George Smart! Oh! he play'd a Consarto,
    With his four-and-twenty fiddlers all on a row!

Then the Lord Archbishop held a goulden dish up,
    For to resave her bounty and great wealth,
Saying "Plase your Glory, great Queen Vict-ory.
    Ye'll give the Clargy lave to dhrink your health!"
Then his Riverence, retrating, discoorsed the mating,
    "Boys! Here's your Queen! deny it if you can!
And if any bould traitour, or infarior craythur,
    Sneezes at that, I'd like to see the man!"

Then the Nobles kneeling to the Pow'rs appealing,
    "Heaven send your Majesty a glorious reign!"
And Sir Claudius Hunter he did confront her,
    All in his scarlet gown and goulden chain.
The great Lord May'r, too, sat in his chair too,
    But mighty sarious, looking fit to cry,
For the Earl of Surrey, all in his hurry
    Throwing the thirteens, hit him in his eye.

Then there was preaching, and good store of speeching,
    With Dukes and Marquises on bended knee;
And they did splash her with raal Macasshur,
    And the Queen said, "Ah! then, thank ye all for me!"—
Then the trumpets braying, and the organ playing,
    And sweet trombones with their silver tones,
But Lord Rolle was rolling;—'twas mighty consoling
    To think his Lordship did not break his bones.

Then the crames and the custards, and the beef and mustard,
   All on the tombstones like a poulterer's shop,
With lobsters and white-bait, and other swate-meats,
   And wine, and nagus, and Imparial Pop!
There was cakes and apples in all the Chapels,
   With fine polonies, and rich mellow pears,
Och! the Count Von Strogonoff, sure he got prog enough,
   The sly ould Divil, underneath the stairs.

Then the cannons thunder'd, and the people wonder'd,
   Crying, "God save Victoria, our Royal Queen!"
Och! if myself should live to be a hundred,
   Sure it's the proudest day that I'll have seen!
And now I've ended, what I pretended,
   This narration splendid in swate poe-thry,
Ye dear bewitcher, just hand the pitcher,
   Faith, it's meself that's getting mighty dhry!

Having come to an end, I paused. Emily, who had made several attempts to interrupt me, but had been checked by an occasional look from me, now burst forth into a torrent of speech.

"Heavens!" she cried. "I am more puzzled than ever. The vulgar creature's account of the procession is perfectly exact. Do you not remember, Fanny, how we admired Prince Esterhazy, so covered with pearls that one could have said he was a knight in coat of mail of jewels?"

"Yes, indeed," I replied, "his narrative appears to tally exactly with our own impression of that eventful day. But how ignorant the fellow is! He calls the Prince de Putbus the Prince of Potboys. Surely Mr. Tom Ingoldsby could not be guilty of such a solecism."

"And surely his brother-in-law's man, that Irish servant of Charles Seaforth's, could never have got into the Abbey. I must ask Tom Ingoldsby about it when we next meet. But Fanny, does it not bring it all back to you, that mad, delightful month we spent in London, in the summer of the Coronation, when I through you and you through me became acquainted with our future husbands."

"We were indeed wild young things then, Emily," said I with a sigh. "How we expected to find one of our dear Boz's characters at every street corner! How we thrilled over the great balloon! How we squeezed and jammed to get to our seats for the procession! How very angry my dear Papa was when we went to see Fanny Elsler dance!"

"And who would have thought then," said Emily, almost mournfully, "that but two years later I would be engaged to be married to your brother, and you would be the mother of your dear little Victoria, who will doubtless be by no means the last."

Provoked at this way of alluding to my future hopes, I was about to retort with one of my more crushing remarks, when a manly footstep in the passage outside caused us both to start.

"Give me the book," cried Emily in a whisper, "and I will keep it at the Rectory, where Mr. Darnley will never see it."

"No indeed," cried I in my turn, indignantly. "It is not your book, Emily. Give it to me."

Another regrettable incident then occurred. Emily retained two pages (luckily they were only the preface) in her grasp, while I thrust the book, mangled but my own, into a large bag of tapestry work in which I carried my sewing; sewing, I may say, of a minute nature, and undertaken with a view to the future rather than the present.

Mr. Darnley then entered. It is not his habit to make use of the library before dinner except on rare occasions such as the visit of an old college friend for whose company he has no particular wish. On such occasions I have known him leave the entertainment of the visitor to me while he, under pretext of estate business, wiles away an hour or so before dinner in perusing the *Athenaeum* or the *Spectator*. Often have I found one of these two periodicals laid with seeming carelessness over one of the *Comic Novels*, or some other light work. Mr. Darnley's appearance was therefore a warrant that something out of the ordinary had happened.

"Well, my love," were his words to me, after he had greeted Emily, "what next, do you think?"

I replied that I was really at a loss; as indeed I was, for anything might happen next.

"What would you say if I told you that there is talk of the railway being brought to Dover within the next few years?"

Neither of us spoke, for it is very difficult to foretell my dear Henry's views on any subject of public interest, and by speaking too soon, before he has fully made up his mind to which side he will give his support, one is often the innocent cause of his uttering sentiments foreign to his real nature.

"Well, Mrs. Darnley," said Henry, turning to the table on which lay the fatal parcel of books, "have you nothing to say on a matter that may gravely affect us both?"

His harsh words so wounded me that I could not utter a word.

Emily, who is a devoted friend, though sometimes provoking past all belief, seeing my nervous condition, nobly came to the rescue.

"Really, Henry," she cried, "you do not expect Fanny, especially in her present condition, to ride in one of those railway coaches? You will be saying next that the railway is to come through your property."

"I have not yet said that it would not," replied Mr. Darnley, who had by now undone the parcel and was looking through the books, comparing them with a paper that he held in his hand. "The bookseller has not sent a copy of a book that I have heard highly recommended, *The Ingoldsby Legends*. I confess I am curious to see whether it really has any connexion with our friends at Tappington Everard. I was sure I had ordered it, and here is a note of the books in my own hand, but I do not see it in the parcel. I will write to London directly, and when the book arrives, you, my Fanny, shall read it to me in the evenings."

At these words I could not longer restrain my feelings and burst into silent tears. Emily, like the mother bird who flutters before the sportsman to distract his attention from her off-spring, cried out,

"What, Henry! Do you mean that you will let the railway come anywhere near Tapton? Are we to see our fields cut up, our woods burnt by the sparks from those hideous tall chimneys? Will you indeed allow the railway contractors and their horrid Irish navigators to come to this neighbourhood? Think of the effect on the lower orders. We have had trouble enough in the village with Chartists, though I must say that the Wesleyans cause very little annoyance, but what will it be now? Instead of going to church, or even chapel, on Sunday, they will drink, gamble, and probably they will poach your pheasants. And as for the village girls and the servant maids, we shall have the work-house full of natural children in no time."

Mr. Darnley contented himself with looking steadily at Emily.

"Nay, you cannot so put me down," she continued. "Had you visited the poor as I have done in my father's parish, you would know the truth of what I say."

"You are speaking, Emily," said Mr. Darnley with admirable temper, "of subjects beyond you. If this railway runs through my property, I shall be well compensated, and as I have among my friends several highly influential gentlemen in the city, it is probable that I shall also obtain shares in the projected under-taking, and be able to support my family in even more comfort than I have hitherto been able to give them."

"Lassy me!" exclaimed Emily, who certainly does use the oddest expressions. "Then you can put a new kitchen range into the Rectory, for I am sure we need one. Farewell, my dearest Fanny."

Before Henry could ring for the footman to show her out, she had glided from the room, and we shortly saw her walking across the terrace towards the Rectory.

"I sometimes feel," said Mr. Darnley, "that Emily is hardly

the wife for a young rector. But doubtless your brother Ned will form and improve her character. Why these tears, my love? Come, let us go upstairs, for it is nearly time to dress for dinner. I will carry your work-bag myself."

My feelings as Henry picked up the bag, repository of my guilty secret, may be imagined. Luckily he suspected nothing, and when alone in my room I locked it safely away in my desk.

A few weeks later Mr. Darnley was obliged to go to Canterbury on some business arising from those wretched riots of two years ago. During his absence I took the opportunity of reading Mr. T. Ingoldsby's book, and so vividly did the poem beforementioned bring back to me the events of the summer of 1838, that I determined to employ my leisure in writing what I could recollect of that year. Luckily the letters which I had written to my dear Mamma had been preserved and sent to me after her lamented death, so I am able to refresh my memory from them. When I think of all the letters I wrote during that period I wonder that I was not ruined in steel nibs. But then anyone who was anyone could get their letters franked. Now that franking has been abolished, the exchange of letters between friends and relatives in various parts of the country will undoubtedly decrease greatly. It is true that there is the new Penny Postage, but there is something low about a thing that every farmer's daughter can afford.

No, my days of letter writing are past, and I shall now employ myself in writing down for my dear Victoria, namesake of our young Queen, though personally unknown to Her Majesty, a mother's memories of the great Coronation year of 1838.

CHAPTER 2

I VISIT THE METROPOLIS

Let me first give a brief account of myself and my family, as it will be through their eyes that this period of history will be seen. My father, Mr. Harcourt, was at that period a gentleman of independent means, living in Norfolk. Here, with the help of my mother, whose weak state of health, however, prevented her from taking any very active part in our education, nor would my father have permitted it even had her health been more robust, myself, my elder brother Ned, and my younger brother William passed our childish days. My parents lived in handsome style and no expense was spared in our education. My brother Ned was at this time, that is in the year 1838, in his third year at Magdalene College, Cambridge. My brother William was at Eton and about to proceed to Christ Church, Oxford, and subsequently to study law. My father had wished to send him to Magdalene, to follow Ned, but William, a youth of determined character, had acquired some prejudice against Cambridge and said that rather than enter that haunt of learning he would go to London, to that very low Radical place, the new London University. At this defiance of his authority my dear father was quite beside himself with rage. At length more reasonable counsels prevailed. It was discovered that my father thought that William, by entering the University of Oxford, was bound sooner or later to be perverted to the Romish faith, but on finding that in order to matriculate William must subscribe to the Thirty-nine Articles, his fury abated, much to all our comfort. For, as he very truly observed, at least at Oxford William would not have to move among Dissenters, and as for the Wesleyans that go there, they are quite a gentlemanly kind of person, and staunch supporters of our Constitution. Thus Passion's reign came to an end and Peace, the smiling and serene, spread her downy wings in our home.

As for myself, by the time I was seventeen I had so well succeeded in keeping six successive governesses in their places, that my parents, anxious for my good, resolved to send me to a boarding-school for a year. The school chosen was Miss Twinkleton's school at Cloisterham, and here it was that I had the good fortune to meet Emily Dacre, motherless daughter and only child of the aged Rector of Tapton, also in the county of Kent. With Emily I formed a bond of attachment that has never weakened, though it has sometimes been sorely tried by Emily's provoking ways. It was while at school that the overpowering news of the death of our Sailor King and the accession of the young Queen Victoria, a girl scarcely older than ourselves, was received. How vividly were our imaginations affected by this event! How often did we again enact the scene at Kensington Palace, myself in my dressing-gown taking the part of the young Queen, and others of my companions assuming for the nonce the characters of the Archbishop of Canterbury and the Lord Chamberlain, until Authority intervened and stopped these representations.

Emily and I vowed solemnly that in the following year, when the Coronation was to take place, we would give our respective parents, or in her case parent, no rest till we had persuaded them to take us to London to see that festivity.

When I went home at Christmas, a young lady prepared to enter the world, I therefore spared no pains to persuade my father and mother that a visit to the metropolis was but suitable to people in their position. To my mother the hope of visiting William at Eton, and receiving a visit in London from her beloved Ned were attractions enough. Alas, that she could not see these wishes fulfilled! My father, like every father that I have ever heard of, made an outcry about the cost of such an expedition, but an appeal to his loyalty was not in vain, and the thought of seeing William at Eton, where he himself had been, was not unpleasant. My dear Emily, who was visiting us for Christmas, added her entreaties to mine, and as she had frequently visited London with her father, who held a senior cardinal's stall in St. Paul's Cathedral, she undertook to procure lodgings for us. All was thus in train for our visit.

Had I known then that my dear papa was spending the capital of his considerable fortune and would, after my mother's death, have barely enough left to live on himself, with no prospect of doing anything for Ned or William, I might not have pressed him so fervently to take us to town. But who can foretell the future? Who could have foreseen that Ned, brought up as the heir to a fortune, would find himself obliged to take orders? Not that the prospect was in any way unpleasant to him, for a country life is quite in his style, and I daresay he will perform the duties at Tapton at least as well as anyone else. Luckily he is to have a curate who will take the major part of the duties, and there is so far but little dissent or poverty in the village. William, having, much to my father's annoyance, come into a little money at the death of his mother, is continuing his studies for the Law and is spoken of as likely to do well. He intends to enter a firm in Doctors' Commons, and it will doubtless solace his hours of study to remember that it is here that our dear Boz makes Alfred Jingle procure the marriage licence to marry the old maid Rachael Wardle. But I may say that my dear father would never have denied himself anything on which he had set his heart, so we should doubtless have gone to London in any case.

As for myself, my dear Mr. Darnley has done everything that is handsome, just as though I had come to him with the large portion that he might have been justified in expecting, and has made a very good settlement on me in the event of his predeceasing me. My brothers will always be welcome here, and as for Papa, though it would be my pleasure as well as my duty to receive him, the expense of the journey is luckily a consideration which, combined with his gout, as I said before, will probably keep him at a distance where affection can still hold her sway, unchecked by propinquity.

The winter and spring passed rapidly away. My parents took me to Norwich from time to time to see the actors at the Theatre Royal, or to balls given for or by the military at the Assembly Rooms. The drive of fourteen miles to our home in the early hours of the morning was not too long when enlivened by the remembrance of an arm pressing my waist, or a flower from my bouquet begged for and bestowed. My mother, alas, was usually unable to attend these festive gatherings, as the illness which finally reft her from us and which prevented her from accompanying us to London was already in possession of her frame.

Nor did I, in the midst of these distractions, neglect my studies. My voice, which though not powerful is said to be sweet and true, was exercised in our English melodies, for my father would hear of no other, while what slight talent I may have had for water-colour drawing was fostered under a pupil of the celebrated Cotman, one of whose later drawings, a view in Norfolk near my old home, was purchased by Mr. Darnley and now hangs in my morning room. I flatter myself that my own efforts, though they are but those of one of the weaker sex, do not compare unfavourably with the works of the professional artist.

It was decided that we were to take rooms for six weeks in London, from the middle of May to the end of June. Emily had procured for us, on very reasonable terms, apartments over a shop in Queen Street, Mayfair. My father had intended to take myself and my mother to London, but a fortnight before our departure a blow fell on me. My dear mother was overcome by a more than usually violent access of her malady, and all was in confusion. My father sent a groom on his best horse to Norwich to require the attendance of the physician who usually attended us, but he had been called away to a confinement at some distance, and could not possibly reach us till the following day. When the groom returned with the message my father flew into such a transport of rage as frightened the poor fellow almost out of his wits. D——d blockhead was the least harsh of the words he used, and indeed he went so far as to threaten the unlucky groom with the treadmill, being a respected county magistrate.

"Papa," I cried, for I had been listening with horror to the painful scene, and my poor mother's sufferings were becoming every moment more acute, "why do you not send for Mr. Perch, the apothecary in the village? He is a very respectable person, and has frequently attended Lady D.'s upper servants. At such a moment we cannot stand on ceremony."

My dear father then made use of an expression relating to Lady D. and her servants and a certain sable gentleman, which I will not repeat. After he had stormed and raged and dismissed all the servants, who were, however, well used to what they called the master's tantrums, he at length consented to send for Mr. Perch, who after examining my mother, announced that her indisposition was of a kind that would make it impossible for her to visit London without grave risk. The Norwich physician confirmed this view, I resigned myself to the inevitable disappointment, and shutting myself up in my room wrote a long letter to my dear Emily, acquainting her with the sad news. My mother, however, displayed her usual sweet unselfishness and insisted that my father and myself should go to town without her, provided that Emily's father would consent to allow her to be our guest in Queen Street, so that we might act as mutual chaperones. Thanking my mother warmly I hastily added a postscript to my letter to Emily, acquainting her with the change in our plans and imploring her to obtain her father's consent. Within a few days I received a reply from her in the affirmative.

"My father," she wrote, "has the utmost dislike of crowds and

PARRIS'S ADMIRABLE DESIGN
OF 'JEALOUSY'

DORLINGS' OFFICIAL AND CORRECT CARD.

W. DORLING & SON, PRINTERS of the Official Cards and Lists, again beg leave to caution the Public against the imposition practised by Vendors in substituting imperfect and spurious Cards for theirs.—☞ See that the Name of " DORLING " is printed on the front and back of each Card.——THE LISTS are filled up and reprinted immediately after the DERBY and OAKS, with the names of the Winners and other particulars. Sold at DORLINGS' *Library and Printing-Office,* EPSOM, and at DORLINGS' STATION ON THE COURSE, *in front of the Grand Stand.*

☞ The Lists of the entry of the **183** Horses for the DERBY, and **117** for the OAKS, for next year, (1842), with all the Winners of former, be immediately printed, and kept on sale throughout the year :—sent post free to all parts of the Kingdom, on receipt of Sixpence in a prepaid

THE CARD OF THE COURSE FOR THE DERBY

noise, and will be only too glad to remain in Tapton, though being the most indulgent of fathers, he was prepared to sacrifice his pleasure to mine and take me to town. A neighbour of ours, a Mr. Henry Darnley, who is travelling to London next week, has offered to take me in his chariot, an invitation which my father has allowed me to accept, the two families having long been on friendly terms, provided that our housekeeper, Mrs. Botherby (daughter of the housekeeper at our friends' the Ingoldsbys), rides in the dickey with Mr. Darnley's man. I therefore expect, dearest Fanny, to be at your door in Queen Street next Wednesday at about half after three. To embrace you again and to hear of your many Norfolk conquests is the dearest wish of your ever affectionate Emily Dacre.

"P.S. Mrs. Botherby will, of course, not remain with me. She is to spend the night with a niece and return on the following day by the coach.

"P.P.S. Mr. Darnley is, I believe, acquainted with your brother, Mr. Ned Harcourt, of whom you have so often spoken to me. He was at Magdalene College and is, like your brother, devoted to aquatic exercises. It is indeed to take part in some rowing match that he is coming to London. What will you think of him, I wonder, my dearest Fanny? And what does your Emily think of him? Ah! ask me not! Thine, E.D."

"As if I should think anything at all of this Mr. Darnley," said I to myself, tossing my head as I refolded Emily's letter. "Another of Ned's horrid, fast rowing friends, I have no doubt. Emily is welcome to him, with all my heart."

How often do we utter in moments of lightheartedness sentiments which riper experience bids us forswear! Had I known then—but which of us knows what lies before him?

It was a fine forward spring. The chestnuts were in full bloom by the first week in May and the strawberry crop promised well. Sadly, yet not without a feeling of pleasurable anticipation, I bade farewell to each favourite nook in garden and field. On the evening before we were to take our departure my father sent for me to his library, a summons I attended with some trepidation, for rarely did a visit to that sanctum mean anything but misunderstanding on Papa's part and indignant tears on mine. I therefore entered prepared to defend myself, whether guilty or innocent. Papa's first words were not calculated to reassure me.

"Well, Fanny," he began, "I suppose you will be needing some fine new gowns to see the Queen, though what the devil you misses want with all these frills and flounces I do not know. You will only be squeezed and flattened in the crowd and no one a penny the wiser of what you are wearing. I dare say I shall have a swingeing bill from your modiste, or what-the-devil-d'you-call-'um, in Norwich for all those balls you went to last winter."

"Indeed, sir," I replied, "I did but have the one new dress, the pink silk with the trimming of rosebuds which Colonel Sparker so much admired. The others were but turned and refurbished, and certainly no one could be more studious of my Papa's purse than I am."

Here injured pride reduced me to loud sobs.

"There, there, my girl," said my father, giving me one of those hearty kisses which are so destructive of filial affection; but my dutiful feelings as a daughter towards my Papa were restored in full when he presented me at the same time with a twenty-pound note for purchases in London. My gratitude may be imagined; and escaping with what grace I could from his affectionate embrace, I sought my room, where my fancy was able to run riot in silks, blonde, mousseline de laine, bonnets with ribbons and marabout, kid gloves, and all the attractions of fashion.

At length the long-looked-for day arrived. My father and myself entered our coach, and with no mishaps arrived in London, my father vowing at every jolt that he would purchase in town a barouche which would be more commodious and also convenient for our country visitings. It was already growing dark when, at about half-past nine o'clock in the evening, we entered the great metropolis, which I had already traversed more than once in going to and returning from Cloisterham. I must confess that my impressions were not altogether pleasant. A strong wind was blowing which filled our coach with dust, straws, and pieces of paper. The noise of coaches, cabs, and drays, was overpowering, and the brilliance of the gas lighting produced an effect almost of terror. As we drove through the streets my father kindly pointed out the principal objects of interest to me, but as it was some twenty years since he had visited London and it was now almost dark except for the gas, and many improvements and changes had been made since that time, his attempts to act as cicerone resulted in a total confusion and loss of temper, so that I privately resolved to make myself acquainted with the public buildings and places of historical celebrity in the company of my dear Emily, when my Papa was otherwise engaged.

As we approached Oxford Street we were stopped by a great concourse of coaches and chariots, with much noise and shouting. In vain did I implore my dear father to bid Bevan (the name of our coachman) turn the horses' heads into some quieter street and so reach our destination; the mere hint of a wish from me was enough to set him off in one of his contrary moods, and letting down the window he halloo'd to Bevan, as though hunting his favourite the fox, telling him to drive on as quickly as possible, that he might see what they had been doing in London. Upon this a couple of very vulgar young men began to quiz him, calling out as nearly as I can reproduce their horrid speech, that he was "vun of the snobs." Then, looking most impertinently in at the coach window one of them put his finger to the side of his nose and winked at me, saying: "Don't you take no manner of notice of Bill, miss. He's only a warmint. You wants a genteel cove like me."

Luckily, just at this moment one of the new policeman came up and laying a hand on the speaker's shoulder told him to "move on," upon which both young men "dispersed themselves," as Mr. Charles Seaforth's Irish servant says. I would willingly have thanked him for his prompt help, but at this moment the obstacle, whatever it was, was removed. I heard some one say in the crowd that it was a poor man fallen down in a faint from hunger, which is very shocking, but others said that it was a horse down, and that its driver had been forced to light some straw under its belly to make it get up. However this may be, our coach was now able to move on. By this time my spirits were so fluttered and exhausted that I had no wish to see any more of the London streets. I was sensible that the coach moved more easily over the pavement of Oxford Street, a fact which my father explained by telling me that the street was now paved with wood, a circumstance which, being a novelty since his younger days, seemed to fill him with rage. At last the coach drew up at the door of 25 Queen Street.

Here a respectable middle-aged person in black, whom I discovered later to be our landlady, Mrs. Bellows, opened the door, and with many curtsys led us to our apartments. We found ourselves in possession of a well-furnished sitting-room on the first floor, looking out into the street, with a dining-room behind it. On the second floor Emily and myself shared the front bedroom, while my father slept at the back, and there was a third bedroom for Ned or any other visitor we might choose to invite. Bevan was to sleep in the mews where the horses were stabled and the coach put up, while Matthews, the footman whom we had brought with us, was comfortably disposed in a closet somewhere under the stairs, and my maid Upton some-where in the attics.

Candles were quickly lighted and Mrs. Bellows inquired whether we chose to take any refreshment. But as it was by now late and my head ached sadly, I refused, merely begging for a cup of tea. The urn was accordingly brought, and seldom was the sound of the boiling water, hissing from the heater, more grate-ful, as I revived my flagging spirits with hyson and pekoe. My father had intended to pass the first evening at his club, White's, but I dissuaded him, alleging the lateness of the hour, though in reality my reason was that he would probably return very late and certainly not in a state of complete sobriety. So ringing for my maid, I betook myself to my bed.

On the following morning I was awoken by the sound of voices below my window. At first I thought I was in my own bedroom in Norfolk and that some of the indoor and outdoor servants were indulging in their own form of merriment. As by degrees my senses grew clearer I perceived that I was in a strange bed and all came back to me. The noises must clearly come from the street below, and being naturally of an inquiring disposition I sprang from my bed and hastily throwing a wrapper round me (did a thought of our young Queen on the day of her accession cross my mind at this moment? Reader, it did!) I ran to the window, drew the curtains, and flung up the sash. Below me an individual in a fan-tailed hat and very dirty red-plush smalls was talking over the area railings to a servant girl whom I took to be the kitchen maid, a small wizened sort of creature. As she was directly below me I could not see her features, but her voice was of that peculiar kind which distinguishes the real Cockney.

"Dustman!" cried the servant girl, "vill you grant me vun pertickler favour?"

The gallant dustman, bending over the area railings, made answer:

"Vy, yes, ma'am, it's unpossible to refuse vun of the soft sex, so I'll consent, pervising as you don't ask me to do nuffin but vot's up right and down straight."

"I vish I may go to blazes," returned the servant, with some spirit, "if it ain't as right as a trivet. Our dusthole ain't been emptied this week—so all the stuff is running into the sile and stopping up the shore, and it's gallus hard lines as ve should be obligated to have sich a muck, and missus isn't on the rampage about it, oh no, not half!"

"Well, miss, it's this way, d'ye see," answered the dustman. "I'm one of them they calls the flying dustmen, and the reg'lar dustmen are all flummoxed and desp'rate 'cos they count as how we takes their reg'lar dust and makes a profit that ought to be going into their pockets. Howsomedever, to oblige a lady, I don't mind emptying your dusthole, hoping that the reg'lar coves aren't anywhere on this beat."

While this conversation was going on I had observed the stealthy approach from the other end of the street of an individual in his shirt sleeves, wearing a dirty white apron. Just as the first speaker was preparing to descend the area steps, the fellow in the apron gave a shrill whistle, at the same time grappling with him. Upon this there appeared round the corner another fellow wearing a full-bottomed fantail hat, breeches of blue plush adorned with mother-of-pearl buttons, red gaiters, and a yellow neckerchief knotted round his neck. He was followed by one of our new Guardians of the Law, who moved in an imposing way, refusing to be hurried in the exercise of his duty.

Seeing that the fellow in the apron was attempting to struggle with the red-plush dustman, the policeman slightly hastened his majestic pace and separating the combatants asked "what the game was?"

"Vy," said the personage in blue plush inexpressibles, "this here consarn is the wery first hoffence as we've been able to conwict this here waggerbone on, but I'll bet a farden cake as he's been a-coming this here horspicious game of dust prigging, till us poor cripples vot follows the dusting line is almost total ruinated."

His complaint was cut short by the policeman, who requested him "not to give him a very long story."

"Now, my man," said he to the red-plush dustman, "you stand there, agin the railings and don't try to give me the slip or I'll run you in. And now, you two others, what's this here precious game?"

"Vy, constable," said the blue-plush fellow, "ven ve finds these here dust-priggers a-taking away the dust vot is lawfully ours, vy, ve naterally laid awake for the criminal. So vot does my matey do this werry identical morning, but voshes the sut bang off his

wisage and claps on a clean vite apron, for to gammon as how he
vos a vaiter, or summut of that 'ere sort—and then he plants
hisself bang again the corner of the street and keeps a sharp look
out for the depredating warmint. Vell, he hadn't been there
more 'an a minnit from this here present moment of time, ven he
cotches this here werry hidentical himperent hindiwidual in the
howdashioustest himperentest way as nobody never seed, go
slap up to the gemman's dusthole and try to fill his bag full of the
gemman's stuff, vich should rightly be mine and my mates'. My
matey gives me the office, and I bolts out, and he bolts out, and
just like vinking ve lays hold of this here werry warmint as
stands—Vy, strike me lucky if he ain't vanished!"

And so, indeed, he had. While the policeman was listening to
the blue-breeched dustman's tale of woe, the red-plush fellow
had taken to his heels and was by now well round the corner of
the street. The policeman, feeling it below his dignity to run in
chase of such a "warmint," contented himself with going to the
corner and looking round, after which he returned to his beat
and left the two regular dustmen to lament their injuries. I must
have laughed with injudicious loudness at this episode, for the
policeman, as he passed under my window, looked up and
grinned at me, which so shocked me, being caught looking out
of a window in my wrapper, that I hastily slammed down the
window and rang the bell for Upton to help me to dress.

Upton when she arrived was in no very good temper, complaining of having been disturbed in her slumbers by creatures of
whose existence I had heard, but whose forms I have never, I am
glad to say, viewed. I therefore told her to make her complaints
to Mrs. Bellows and not to me, and descended to the dining-
room for breakfast.

Mrs. Bellows was in attendance to see whether I required
anything, so I mentioned to her the occurrence I had just
witnessed, and asked her the meaning of it. She then told me
that the regular dustmen were much annoyed in their work by
the piratical behaviour of unlicensed men, known as "flying

dustmen," who, making themselves acquainted with the houses where the dustholes had not been lately emptied, offer to remove the unpleasant accumulation for the householder, an offer which is gladly accepted; for the servant's statement about the refuse getting into the sewers, or shores as she called them, was, so my informant told me, perfectly correct.

"And what we would do, miss, without the flying dustmen, I really couldn't say," added Mrs. Bellows. "They are a blessing in disguise, look at it which way you will, and then those police have to come interfering as if this wasn't a free country."

I then learned, which surprised me excessively, that the regular dustmen sometimes make vast fortunes out of the refuse that they collect. They carry it away to some piece of waste ground and there go through it for what valuables they may find, selling bones, fat, and such kitchen offal, which always find a ready market (though for what purpose I cannot conceive) and finding purchasers, strange as it may appear, for rags, old paper, and the thousand things that are thrown away in the kitchen. I could not help thinking as I reviewed the scene of the morning and the surprising facts narrated to me by Mrs. Bellows, what a story this would make for Mr. Dickens. He, who is so fond of the oddities of London life and so well portrays low characters, might find excellent material in the life of one of these dustmen who turns refuse to gold.

Mrs. Bellows, I found, was but too ready to gossip on any subject. She said she was housekeeper to a nobleman till her marriage, when she bought this house—from her savings as she says, but I cannot but suspect that the nobleman in question made her a *handsome* wedding present—and took in lodgers. Queen Street has had more than one householder of doubtful respectability, it appears, in spite of its fashionable situation and the houses of the aristocracy which surround it on every side. Mrs. Bellows had already dropped dark hints about a certain family called Dubochet, who exercised the trade of stocking mending, which have excited my lively curiosity. I must learn more about this family, several of whose members appear to have been *intimately* acquainted with the most exclusive members of the aristocracy at the time when Mrs. Bellows first came to Queen Street.

CHAPTER 3

OXONIAN AND CANTABS

My first and natural impulse was of course to go out and view some of the sights of London, but my father being engaged on business all day, and my own feelings of propriety telling me that though he would be none the wiser if I went out in his absence, I might lose my way, or be exposed to some such annoyances as I had experienced in the coach on the previous day, I resolved to stay in our lodgings, and Upton still being in the sulks, I employed myself in writing to my dear mother and looking out of the window at the equipages and the passers-by. Mrs. Bellows coming up with some message and finding me thus engaged, asked me whether I were not afraid of catching cold.

"Indeed, no, Mrs. Bellows," said I, "the air is warm and nothing can be more pleasant than to see what is happening in the street. Look, for example, at that gentleman, who is now walking up the opposite side of the road. He must be one of the famous dandies!"

Mrs. Bellows approached the window and looked out. The gentleman whom I had pointed out to her appeared to be of about thirty years of age. Though formed in manly mould his face was of an interesting pallor. Black clustering curls escaped from beneath his hat, and his dress was of the highest elegance, from his lavender gloves to his varnished boots. His attention had doubtless been attracted by the sound of our voices, for as he passed in front of the house he looked up. His large and expressive eyes seemed to pierce my very mind, and I thought that a faint sneer of contempt curled his finely chiselled nostril. He then averted his gaze, resumed his saunter, and was presently lost to view.

At this moment I keenly felt the indelicacy of my conduct in having attracted the attention of a stranger of the opposite sex, and I reflected how extremely embarrassing it would be if we should ever meet again. Yet I could not altogether banish the hope that chance might bring us together. There was something wild and romantic about his pale face and dark eyes which played strangely upon my fancy.

"Imperent young man," said Mrs. Bellows, drawing me away from the window. "Come inside, miss. I can see you don't know London. Why, for two pins the young fellow would have bowed to you. I could see he was struck all of a heap. You can't be too careful, miss. There may be chance meetings that lead to all sorts of things that I wouldn't mention to a young lady like you. That was the way the family I was telling you about became so notorious, miss. Their father, Mr. Dubochet, a Swiss he said he was, but there, all those foreigners are alike, kept a shop for mending stockings at number twenty-three, and the girls were up and down the street morning, noon, and night. There used to be a lot of fine young gentlemen always hanging about, particularly an Honourable Mr. Craven who lived at the big house you can see, miss, if you put your head out of the window, with the obbylicks at the front door. One of the girls ran away with this young gentleman's brother and took the name of Harriette Wilson. A lively little thing she was, I remember her well, no beauty, but she had a way with the gentlemen, and a kind heart. Well, no one knows what has become of her now. But if she and her sister hadn't looked out of the window so much, many things mightn't have happened, though one of them did marry a real lord."

"Well, Mrs. Bellows," said I, "if looking out of the window is to catch me a lord for a husband, perhaps I may look again."

So saying, I returned to the window, when to my astonishment I saw my Unknown turning the corner into Queen Street again. Surprise and curiosity held me rooted to the ground while he passed, once more raising his eyes with a fixed gaze to my face. Half gratified, half ashamed, I withdrew and resumed my writing, though with a fluttering at my heart which I could not still.

However, not long afterwards all my dreams were not unpleasantly dispelled by a loud ringing at the door-bell, a hurried rush of steps on the stairs, and the entrance of my brother Ned. So much news had we to exchange that we could scarcely hear one another speak. After showing a proper though somewhat hurried interest in our mother's illness, Ned informed me that he had got two nights' leave from Cambridge and would be coming up to London later for a longer period. It appeared that he was engaged, with some of the other Under Graduates, to take part in a race upon the river against a club of oarsmen named Leander.

"It will be famous sport, Fanny," he cried. "Last year we had a match against the Leander club, famous rowing men they are, and we beat them hollow. So this year they challenged us to a return match, and though very few on the river can go their pace, I have no doubt we shall whop them finely. Our fellows are all coming to town shortly to practise for the race, and then I warrant you'll see something worth seeing."

"How truly delightful, dear Ned," said I. "But I fear your friends must be a terribly fast set. Rowing men always are."

At this insinuation Ned became quite indignant, and then held forth at such length and so very boringly about watermen and oars and strokes that my thoughts withdrew into themselves once more and played fancifully about the Unknown, till I was roused by a second violent ringing at the front door-bell and more steps on the stairs. It was Emily Dacre.

Confused at not finding me alone she stopped in the doorway, and though I prefer for my part a more refined and ethereal type of beauty than dear Emily's, I must confess that she looked vastly well in her green silk walking dress and hat. I flew to her arms, and when our mutual transports had subsided I presented Ned to her.

"Nay, Mr. Ned Harcourt," said she archly, "we are not strangers. I even know your name, you see. Your sister's partiality to a beloved brother has made it familiar to my ears."

Ned, who is no ladies' man, muttered something about "honoured and obliged" and "necessity of taking his leave."

"Besides," added Emily, "the gentleman, an old friend of my family's, who was kind enough to offer me and my maid a seat in his chariot today, is also, I believe, a Cambridge acquaintance of yours, Mr. Henry Darnley."

"God bless my soul," cried Ned. "Hal Darnley? Where is he?"

Without waiting for an answer, or so much as apologizing for his coarse expression, he bounded to the window and threw up the sash, shouting, "Hal, my good fellow, come upstairs!"

"Mr. Ned is so delightfully natural," said Emily to me, "But really I am quite embarrassed. If Mr. Darnley thought it was on my account that he was invited upstairs, I should sink through the ground with confusion."

"Rest assured, my love," said I, "that if Ned and this Mr. Darnley were at Cambridge together, they will prose away by the hour and take no notice of our charms."

Emily appeared a little piqued by my remark, but at this moment Mr. Darnley entered the room. In him I beheld a tall young man, well made and active, dressed in quiet but gentlemanly taste. His face, which would otherwise have been not ill looking, was somewhat marred by a nose which appeared to have felt the effects of the pugilist's art. His manner when introduced was easy but respectful, and I thought I could detect in it a certain pleasure at finding two members of the opposite sex.

"I must tell you, ladies," said he when we were seated, "that Ned here is my deadly enemy for at least three weeks to come. Since I came down from Cambridge I have had the honour to be elected to the Leander club which is to meet the Cambridge Under Graduates in a match upon the river in June. But I fear for our reputation, for we are an elderly set compared with these young bloods."

"That is all very well, Hal," cried Ned, "but you have practised together. In our crew there are but two from the same college, and all row in different styles. I can tell you, Noulton will have to damn and curse us up and down the river to get us to his liking."

"Noulton," said Mr. Darnley, "is the best waterman and the best coxswain on the river here except for our waterman, Parish, so I dare say that all will be even enough. But this conversation, Ned, can have but little interest for Miss Harcourt and Miss Dacre."

Ned, quite undeterred by being so pointedly set down, continued to talk with great spirit about the match, but Mr. Darnley, with the polished ease of a man of the world, insensibly led the conversation to the theatre, the opera, and the charms of literature, so that the time passed very agreeably, Ned sitting half asleep in an arm-chair, till the gentlemen rose to take their leave. Mr. Darnley offered to drive Ned in his chariot wherever he wished to go, and begged to be allowed the honour of calling upon us again soon.

When he had gone Emily became so unbearably simpering and affected in her talk about him that friendship was strained in a manner which could only be repaired by an inspection of our joint wardrobes and a discussion of the purchases we wished to make.

My father presently came home and welcomed Emily with his usual boisterous heartiness. He informed us that he had some very welcome news. It appeared that going into town to make inquiries about seats to view the Coronation procession, he had met the son of an old friend, a young man studying law

in London, who had cordially pressed him to accept two ladies'
tickets for a stand in front of his club, as his mother and sister
who were to have used them were detained in the country by the
illness of a near relation.

"So that's what I call a good stroke of luck," said my father,
"and though the young man is a bit of a puppy, I daresay you
girls won't like him any the worse for that. I say God bless our
young Queen as heartily as any one, and damn all Radicals, but
I'm not going to sit on a bit of board all day for the pleasure of
seeing her. You girls can have that to yourselves. Well, haven't
either of you a kiss for the old Squire for getting you seats and a
young man to keep you company?"

Emily, who, doubtless from her deprivation from early years
of a mother's care, has not all the delicacy that her dearest friends
would wish, kissed my father readily, but I confess that gratitude
was not among the first of my feelings.

"Good heavens, Papa!" I cried. "Will there not be great
impropriety in our accepting these tickets? A young man whom
we do not know? To sit in so exposed a situation as a club? and
without a chaperone?"

Upon this my dear father took great offence, saying I was just
like my mother, and ridiculing what he called my old maid's
notions so unmercifully that tears came to my eyes, and with
very little effort I sobbed aloud.

"There, there, Fan," said my father. "It was but a joke, and you
girls must always turn on the waterworks when no harm is
intended. Mr. Vavasour is coming to take tea with us this
evening with his aunt, and then perhaps your prudery will be
satisfied."

"Lassy me!" cried Emily, "a gentleman to tea? I must make
some change in my toilette," and the giddy creature ran upstairs, followed at a less impetuous pace by the writer of these
Memoirs.

After dinner we sat in the drawing-room and my dear father
desired us to sing. It was a balmy evening. The windows were

open and no breath stirred the air. Mrs. Bellows's pianoforte, though not modern, had by no means an unpleasant tone, and Emily and I mingled our voices in the strains of a duet, to my accompaniment. As the last notes died away, Emily's contralto echoing my soprano voice, Matthews the footman knocked at the door and announced: Mrs. Vavasour and Mr. DeLacy Vavasour.

It was now dusk in the room, so our greetings were exchanged in some confusion and I could only see that Mrs. Vavasour was of middle height, and her nephew tall and slight. While Matthews was lighting the candle I was better able to study my visitors. Mrs. Vavasour was past her first youth, but most lady-like in appearance and tastefully dressed. Her voice was soft and her manner ingratiating, and I felt strongly predisposed towards her. Meanwhile my father had been talking to Mr. DeLacy Vavasour at the other side of the room, and it was not till Mrs. Bellows entered, bearing one of those brilliant Carcel lamps, that I recognized in him my Unknown of the afternoon!

"Good God!" I cried, and then stopped, overcome by emotion and embarrassment.

At the sound of my voice Mr. Vavasour turned and looked towards me. Then with perfect composure he walked over to where I sat and entered into conversation with me and Emily. If I had admired him in the street, how much more admirable did he appear when I could study him closely. His high alabaster forehead was shadowed by dark ringlets, negligently yet becomingly arranged. His Grecian nose was finely chiselled and his mouth expressed sarcasm and feeling. But how can I describe his eyes? Large and lustrous, capable of expressing the tenderest and the sternest emotions, they conveyed a message to me whose meaning I could not mistake. His white hands, with long nervous fingers, played idly with one of the rich gold chains that were twisted about his neck, or were raised now and again to push aside the curls that seemed almost too heavy for his small and well-shaped head.

The conversation, in which I was hardly able to bear my part, presently turned on the approaching Coronation, and when the tea equipage was brought I was thankful to slip into my place behind it and listen in silence. Mrs. Vavasour, in the civilest way possible, begged Emily and myself to consider ourselves as one of her family while we were in London.

"I shall be delighted, Mr. Harcourt," said she, "to chaperone your daughter and Miss Dacre whenever they require my services. I am myself going to see the procession from my nephew's club in Pall Mall, and you may safely trust the young ladies to me."

My father, who is almost invariably polite to females, other than those of his family, thanked her cordially and accepted on our behalf. Mrs. Vavasour then added:

"I hear there is a match to be rowed in June on the river, which will be an entertaining spectacle. My nephew has engaged at my request a cutter with excellent watermen, and we are making up a party to view the race. May I hope that Miss Harcourt and Miss Dacre and yourself will be of our number?"

Forgetting my embarrassment I exclaimed aloud, "How truly delightful! My brother, dear Mrs. Vavasour, is rowing in the match, and it will afford me the greatest pleasure to observe his exertions. Miss Dacre too knows Mr. Darnley, who is taking part."

Emily joined her thanks to mine, and Mrs. Vavasour's face beamed with the pleasure that benevolence alone can impart. I noticed that Mr. Vavasour was silent, and turning to him, my confusion quite forgotten, I asked him whether he thought my brother would win.

His full lip curled with scorn as he answered:

"Miss Harcourt will pardon me if I observe that rowing is hardly a sport in which a man would take a deep interest. A contest in which any gentleman may be overcome by an ignorant waterman is not what a man would choose. Our fellows are not rowing against Cambridge this year, and time will show that they are right in confining their aquatic efforts to their native Isis."

I was bewildered and must have shown it all too clearly, for he added;

"By us, I mean the Oxonians. The Cantabs are so anxious for the vulgar applause of the mob that sooner than forgo a match they are rowing against a private club."

"Are you then an Oxonian?" I asked with some interest, for I had found among Ned's books a volume entitled *The Oxonian*, with coloured plates, which, though highly unsuitable for female reading, had caused me to burn the midnight oil for several evenings, when I knew my dear father was not likely to disturb me.

"I was," he answered smiling, "but for several years I have lived in London, reading law and following the pursuit of literature. Perhaps you may have read some of my novels?"

"I do not know—I fear not—what are their names?" I asked, confused.

"I shall send them to you, if you will allow me," said Mr. Vavasour, and drawing his chair nearer to mine he added in a lower tone:

"Has Miss Harcourt forgiven me my unfortunate boldness of this afternoon?"

"Sir—Mr. Vavasour—I hardly understand you," said I, ready to sink with embarrassment.

"I admire your delicacy," said he, "but between acquaintances, I dare not say friends, who are to be thrown much together in the next few weeks, frankness is essential. Miss Harcourt, this afternoon I was passing down Queen Street. I heard the silvery tone of a voice from an upper window. I looked up. I need not tell you what I saw. Conscious of the impropriety of staring at a lady to whom I was unknown, I tore myself away. But Nature, the wild, the primeval, is strong in us. Hardly had I turned the corner than I was irresistibly drawn to retrace my steps. I dared to look up again. You withdrew from the window, and I was left with the conviction that I had deeply offended one whom I reverenced and admired. I met your father. He invited me to bring my aunt to visit him and his daughter. Imagine my feelings as we entered a house which I recognized to be the happy abode of the vision I had lately seen. Now, I beg you, Miss Harcourt, to tell me that I am forgiven."

His deep manly accents, bearing the stamp of truth, thrilled my nerves. I bowed my head in assent and accidentally managed to drop my handkerchief. He stooped, retrieved it from the carpet, and put it into his bosom. Then, bowing deeply, as though unable to trust himself to speak, he entered into general conversation. Nothing more occurred worthy of notice, and our visitors shortly took their leave.

It was at a late hour that Ned returned, and I heard him as he retired to rest singing loudly:

> "To keep up our wind round the meadows we run,
>   And return with a pain in the liver;
> But what does it matter, my boys, when there's fun
>   To be found every night on the river."

Had he sung this effusion, the remaining words of which I was unable to catch, but once, it would not so have imprinted itself on my memory, but Emily and I, stifling our laughter, heard this ditty, with the addition of many "tol-de-rols" repeated at least twenty times before Morpheus claimed the Cantab for his own.

On the following day Mr. Darnley came to call. My father received him with his customary heartiness, and all was going well till Mr. Darnley happened to mention that he had seen a certain piece of news in the *Weekly Despatch,* upon which my father at once flew into one of his rages, stigmatizing the journal in question as a low, subversive, Radical organ. Mr. Darnley was not backward in defending his views, and a quarrel, if not actual blows, seemed imminent, when Ned, who had hitherto been silent, intervened to make matters worse.

"Pray, Hal," he said, drawing a piece of newspaper from his pocket, "read this, and then defend your Radical friends if you can. Or rather," he continued mischievously, "I will read it aloud, that my father may hear."

In vain did I nod and wink at Ned, who was now in one of the moods when he likes to see cocks or dogs tear each other to pieces, so I contented myself with giving Mr. Darnley a glance expressive of sympathy.

"Here's a pretty piece of writing from the *Weekly Despatch*," said Ned. "The fellow who wrote it is dead against the Coronation and such a bit of clap-trap you never did hear. 'I do most ardently hope,' he says, 'that if the disgusting, superstitious, and blasphemous ceremony of the Coronation is to be inflicted upon us, Mr. Plumtre, or some other member of the House of Commons, will move that the day following this absurd mockery of religion may be observed as a General Fast and Humiliation for our sins, in profaning God's House by a number of men and women assembling to kiss each other in it; by a set of sturdy Bishops unloosing the dress of the Queen to bedaub her body with oil.' Then he adds that the French are far better than we, 'for they continue the religion from which these brutalities arose, whilst the English preserve the brutalities after they have got rid of the superstition.' What do you say to that, Hal?"

"The writer's views are indeed expressed with an unbecoming warmth," was Mr. Darnley's reply, "but any reasoning being must admit the justice of much that he says."

"I'm damned if they must," cried my father, hardly able to contain himself. "French indeed! Why, one Englishman can beat any three Frenchmen! Who is the writer? Who is the atheistical, disloyal scoundrel?"

"Publicola, sir," said Ned.

"A dirty ruffian that skulks behind a name out of the Latin Grammar," said my father. "I wish old Keate had him up for flogging. He would so trounce him that he couldn't sit to write his treasonous rubbish for a week."

"Publicola, Mr. Harcourt," said Mr. Darnley, "does but conceal the name of Mr. Fox, one of our ablest writers."

"Lassy me!" cried Emily, "I thought Mr. Fox dead, lord knows how long ago."

"Well, it's all one," said my father angrily, "Fox is a damned treacherous, revolutionary name. I'd shoot any one called Fox."

"What, sir, would you shoot a fox?" asked Mr. Darnley laughing.

"It's what you and your Radical friends would do," growled my dear father. "I daresay you would give poachers silver spoons to eat your partridge, and pheasants too."

At this Mr. Darnley made a strong protest, and it appeared that his views as a landowner and magistrate were so completely in accord with those of my father and Ned on the subject of poaching that peace reigned once more. I confess I also had thought that Fox was dead, but then politics are entirely beyond me, and I find it does not matter a rap whether one understands them or not, for the gentlemen will talk about them just the same. But I felt, for the first time, that there might be something to be said for the Radicals, if Mr. Darnley was on their side.

Ned now remarked that there was a balloon ascent that evening from the Royal Surrey Zoological Gardens, and made a proposal that we should all go.

"It was famous fun when Mr. Green and Mr. Gye went up in their monster balloon a year or two ago," said Ned. "I was at Vauxhall with a party of fellows and I assure you it was famous. They came down in Russia or Prussia or somewhere, and we all got famously drunk that night."

At this Emily, looking archly at Ned, hummed a line of his song of the previous evening:

But what does it matter, my boys, when there's fun
   To be found every night on the river!

Ned had the grace to look a little ashamed, and hurriedly rang the bell to order a hackney coach, our horses still being tired after the journey. Accordingly we all set out, accompanied by Mr. Darnley. The view of the town as we drove towards Westminster Bridge was truly impressive, and Mr. Darnley was obliging enough to point out to us his club, the Reform, which was a magnificent mansion in Whitehall.

"We are to build a club in Pall Mall," said Mr. Darnley, "which will far surpass our present temporary home. But I hope I may be permitted to offer the hospitality of this building, such as it is, to Miss Harcourt and Miss Dacre, for the purpose of viewing the Coronation procession. Our French cook is to give a magnificent breakfast for about two thousand people, and it will be quite one of the events of the day."

My dear father here said he would be damned if any of his family should set foot in a low Radical Club.

"It is truly kind of you, and I know you will not notice papa," said I, "but I fear we are already engaged to see the procession from the club of Mr. DeLacy Vavasour, a friend of my father's."

"Vavasour who wrote *Jocelyn FitzFulke?*" asked Mr. Darnley.

"I do not know," was my reply. "He said he had written a number of novels, but I am ignorant of their names. He promised, however, that he would send me copies of his works."

Mr. Darnley did not reply. At this moment we were crossing Westminster Bridge and my father pointed out to us the site where the Houses of Parliament had formerly stood until burnt down, a misfortune which he seemed to take very much to heart. Ned, who had been laughing and talking with Emily, drew our attention to the ballast machines in the river outside the House of Lords, where preparations for building were taking place.

"Those coffer dams have set up some strong eddies, Hal," he said, "and we are likely to have trouble when we pass them. It's a lucky job that both crews have watermen that know these reaches of the Thames like their own pockets."

But Mr. Darnley, doubtless feeling that Ned would talk for ever if not checked, described to us in a very lively way the burning of the Houses of Parliament, which he had personally been lucky enough to witness. My father was inclined to ascribe the conflagration to the Radical party, but did not persist. We thus passed by the Obelisk, which reminded me of Mrs. Bellows's "Obbylicks" and as we approached the Zoological Gardens the crowd became so dense that our coach could only proceed with difficulty. It consisted chiefly of the lower classes, and I expressed my fears to Mr. Darnley that we might find ourselves with rather unpleasant neighbours who would jostle or incommode us.

"If any rude fellow presumed to jostle Miss Harcourt," said Mr. Darnley, "it would give me the greatest pleasure."

I looked my astonishment.

"For," added he, "I should then have the pleasure of knocking him down."

"Ay, Hal's a famous bruiser," cried Ned. "You can tell that by his smashed proboscis. He stood up against the Babraham Pet for ten rounds at Cambridge the year I came up."

"Allow me to compliment you, sir," said my father. "There's nothing like the fists for Englishmen, but things are sadly altered now. In my young days we had Mendoza and Belcher and the Game Chicken and a dozen more. Now it's all fighting on the cross."

He then shook hands warmly with Mr. Darnley, and said he was sure the pretty girls would like a young fellow none the worse for having a broken nose.

"I never heard that the shape of a man's nose prevented his kissing a lady," said my father, in high good humour, at which Ned guffawed.

"I dare to say your father is thinking of me," said Emily to me in a whisper, "but he is wrong. The very thought is quite shocking to me."

I did not relish her remark, and merely replied that I was sure my father had no such thing in his mind.

We had by now arrived at the Gardens and alighted. Knowing that my dear father would, as invariably occurs, enter into an altercation with the coachman as to the amount of the fare, Emily and I withdrew to a slight distance. After some high words had passed, attracting the attention of the crowd, my father rejoined us. From his conversation we gathered that he had tendered three shillings to the coachman, who had strongly maintained that his legal fare was four.

"In my young days, the coachman would have fought us for the fare," said my father sadly, "but these fellows are too tame to show fight. I had half a mind to call one of these policemen and give him in charge."

"I believe," said Mr. Darnley mildly, "that he was within his rights in demanding four shillings."

At this Emily pinched Mr. Darnley's arm, nodding so significantly that he said no more, while I, hastening to avert the explosion which I saw to be imminent, asked my father how he had settled the matter.

"I can tell you, Fan," said Ned, interrupting. "The coachman pitched a yarn about a wife and twenty children, and the governor gave him five shillings."

My father growled something about an impudent puppy, but was forced to join in the general laugh and confess that Ned had been right. We then entered the gardens, which were both tasteful and magnificent, statuary with gushing fountains, glass houses for exotic plants, and large cages for the feathered tribes being among their attractions. Emily expressed a wish to see the animals, but it was already getting late, so following the crowd we made our way towards a large piece of ornamental water.

"Never mind, Miss Dacre," said Ned. "I will bring you here another day with Fan, and you shall see the rhinoceros and the giraffes."

"I do long," said Emily, "to see the female gorilla. She must be a doat of an animal. And I would dearly love to see the kangaroos swallow their young."

At this Ned again rudely burst into a loud guffaw, while Mr.

Darnley, pained as I could see by Emily's shocking use of the word female, endeavoured to cover the confusion which she did not feel by relating to me a charming anecdote about a black spaniel, who had strayed by chance into the lion's cage. The King of Beasts, instead of killing the dog, took it under his protection, and fondled and played with it, and when the spaniel died the lion, broken-hearted, did not survive the loss of his companion more than a few days.

I was truly touched by this story and was about to shed a tear, but the crowd became here so thick and noisy that I could only express by a look the interest that I felt. On the opposite side of the lake we could distinguish the yet flaccid form of the balloon. Boats were rowing across the lake with combustibles for the rarefying apparatus which, so Ned said, was to inflate the balloon, and all was bustle and movement. Around us the crowd was becoming restless, several people saying in loud voices that they had paid their money and waited quite long enough, while booings and hisses began to arise in an alarming way. Presently we observed a man putting up placards in various parts of the grounds. Approaching the nearest, what was our disappointment to read as follows:

"The Balloon cannot ascend, but in compensation for the unavoidable disappointment an Eruption will take place at dusk."

The crowd at once began to express its disapprobation of the news by making towards the balloon in a threatening manner. Our party with some little difficulty succeeded in getting to a slight distance, but even from here the sight was truly terrifying. Some threw stones at the boats on the lake, most of which were stove in and sunk. The greater number of the spectators made for the enclosure where the balloon was lying, and smashing down the palings threw themselves upon the unresisting monster. At first they satisfied themselves by pelting it with stones, but their spirits rising with the growing dusk they dragged the balloon to the edge of the lake and tore it to pieces with frenzied shouts. Emily and I, both seriously alarmed, begged my father to take us away, to which he reluctantly agreed, being half inclined to see the frolic through. As we made our way towards the gate two figures passed us, running at full speed with a crowd at their heels. We learnt next day that they were the unlucky owners of the balloon, who had barely escaped with their lives. At last we reached the exit, where a large notice of "Money Returned" was being posted up, but without waiting for our money we passed rapidly out. All was not yet over, however. Two or three very low-looking individuals, a part of the crowd who had been pursuing the unfortunate owners of the balloon, came jostling about us, and one went so far as to offer to "kiss the gals." Emily and I both screamed. At the same moment a hackney coach drove up, and a voice cried, "Get in guv'ner! I'll drive your lordship anyveres after the werry handsome way your lordship treated me."

Without ceremony my father hustled Emily and myself in and jumped in after us, followed by Ned. One of the blackguards was attempting to snatch at my shawl, which hung from the window, when Mr. Darnley very coolly stepped up to him and with a well-directed blow laid him senseless on the ground. He then leapt into the coach, telling the man to drive on, and we were soon out of sight of the crowd, though the light of the Eruption of Vesuvius was for some time plainly visible. The journey home was excessively uncomfortable. Not only were Emily and I in a highly nervous state, but the coachman had undoubtedly been spending part of my father's ill-placed bounty on intoxicating drink, and drove very wildly, causing Emily and myself to shriek at frequent intervals. When we got to Queen Street, Mr. Darnley and Ned took their leave, Mr. Darnley to go to his club, and Ned to spend the night with a Cambridge friend and catch the early coach back to the University.

Emily and I retired to our room, where Emily's way of taking

"BRAVO THE CANTABS!"

it for granted that Mr. Darnley had knocked the man down on her behalf made me quite ashamed of her, and I felt it my duty to tell her so. After all it was *my* shawl that the ruffian had attempted to snatch. We then both burst into tears and went to sleep.

THE PADDINGTON STATION

CHAPTER 4
WE VISIT THE TEMPLES OF ART

For the next few days Emily and I were fully occupied in visiting various modistes and mantua-makers recommended to us by Mrs. Vavasour. Willingly would we have ordered a ball dress each, for the materials were truly ravishing. Especially did we doat upon a dress of white organdy embroidered with sprigs of coloured worsted, a coloured print of which Madame Jupon of Hanover Square had shown to us in a French *Journal des Modes*. It had a very low *corsage en cœur*, long full sleeves, and a *ceinture* of brilliant *gorge de pigeon* silk, and was worn with white silk stockings and black shoes. But prudence prevailed. It was not likely that we should be asked to any grand balls, and though Emily is an heiress, her mother having left her a handsome fortune, I did not feel inclined to let her eclipse me. I therefore persuaded her that a handsome walking dress and dinner dress each would sufficiently replenish our wardrobe, besides hats, kid gloves, brodequins, shawls, and any other trifles we might require.

Accordingly Emily decided upon a walking dress of violet *peau de soie* with a low corsage, and a mantelet of green taffetas trimmed with lace. Her hat of green *peau de soie* was to be trimmed with ribbons and flowers, and formed a deep and becoming frame for her face. For myself I chose a dress of cedar colour *gros de Naples* worn with a very large shawl of *soie chatoyante*, whose mingled shades of blue and green were indeed exquisite. My hat was to be of pink *gros de Naples* with a deep trimming of blonde, ornamented with ribbons and marabout. Madame Jupon promised to have the dresses ready for fitting early in the following week, and with this we were forced to be satisfied.

"I am only too ready to oblige any friend of Mrs. Vavasour's," said Madame Jupon, "but really you have no idea how pressed we are. There is such uncertainty about the Coronation, some saying it will be in June, and others, according to the newspapers, wishing to put it off till August, so that my customers are quite at a loss, for a dress that would be quite *à la mode* in June may not be the latest fashion in August; besides I hear from Paris that hats are getting smaller, and then we shall be left with large stocks on our hands. I do assure you, ladies, I am quite distracted and have had to engage eight more young ladies, some of whom are hardly worth the wages I have to pay. They are at work till eleven or twelve every night, but even so I hardly like to take another order, though, ofcourse, I make an exception for any one introduced to me by Mrs. Vavasour."

Emily's attention was here attracted to a half-finished dress of *mousseline de laine*, embroidered with gay bouquets in silk.

"I see you are looking at that dress," Madame Jupon ran on, "it is one of the most exclusive we have yet made this season. It is for the Lady Almeria Norbourne, a young lady of great fortune and a famous beauty. She is the ward of your friend Mrs. Vavasour, so doubtless you will make her acquaintance. Now, ladies, what can I show you in the way of dinner gowns or evening dresses? I have the very latest patterns from Paris, you will find nothing more modish anywhere. Miss Smith, bring up the yellow muslin and the pink crape for these ladies to see."

"Thank you very much, Madame Jupon," said I, "but I am too fatigued to see anything more today. If your assistants are half as tired as I am, I pity them."

"Oh no, miss," said Madame Jupon, "they are used to it. Miss Smith thinks nothing of it, do you, Miss Smith?"

Miss Smith merely bowed. A faint interest was roused in me by her delicate appearance and the description which Madame Jupon had previously given of the hours of work, but reflecting that I knew nothing of her real situation, nor did I wish to, I took my leave.

"Why did you hurry away so, Fanny?" asked Emily as we walked away.

"I felt such an oppression that I could not stay any longer," was my reply. "Emily, I would like to see Lady Almeria. A beauty and a fortune—and doubtless she is thrown much into Mr. Vavasour's society."

Here I sighed loudly.

"My poor Fanny," replied Emily, tenderly pressing my arm, "I can indeed sympathize with you. But do not let your fancy form too lively images. I too know what it is to feel a flame which I cannot reveal. The other night, after Mr. Darnley's heroic conduct, I could not sleep a wink."

Emily is really insufferable at times. As I said before, it was *my* shawl. Hurrying on to conceal my annoyance, I was nearly knocked over at the corner of Bond Street by a party of ladies and gentlemen proceeding in the opposite direction. I was about to make my apologies, when Emily, pressing forward, greeted them all warmly.

"My dear Fanny," she cried, "here we are indeed among friends. Here is our neighbour Mr. Ingoldsby from Tappington Everard, his son, Mr. Tom Ingoldsby, and his daughter and son-in-law Mr. and Mrs. Charles Seaforth. And this is my friend Miss Harcourt, of whom you have often heard me speak, with whom I am on a visit."

Mutual greetings ensued, and it was decided that we should all go to Gunter's, the pastrycook's in Berkeley Square, and take some ices. As soon as we were settled, the conversation naturally turned upon the approaching Coronation which had brought us all to London. I mentioned that Madame Jupon had read that the ceremony was to be postponed, but old Mr. Ingoldsby pooh-poohed this.

"It is all settled," said he, "for the twenty-eighth of June, and we are going to see it in the Abbey."

"But how will you do that, Mr. Ingoldsby?" asked Emily. "I thought tickets were only to be got through the Earl Marshal's office, and were not transferable."

"That's what the other geese thought," said old Mr. Ingoldsby chuckling, "but we country people aren't such fools as we look. My Tom here has got us tickets from a stationer's in the Strand. There are plenty of fine lords and ladies who are glad to turn an honest penny by selling their places."

"How much did you pay for them, Mr. Ingoldsby?" Emily inquired, with that want of delicacy that is a distinguishing trait of her character.

"Never you mind, my dear," said the old gentleman, with whom Emily seemed to be a great favourite, and chuckling again, "but this I will tell you, that the late-comers will have to pay much more. I wouldn't mind wagering that the price will go up to 50 guineas for some of the seats before the day itself."

"Lassy me!" said Emily.

"You are not the only good bargain-maker, sir," said Mr. Tom Ingoldsby, a satirical-looking young man. "What do you think Thady has done? Thady, I must tell you, Miss Harcourt, is the Irish servant of my brother-in-law Charles here. Miss Dacre knows him and his bulls very well."

"Indeed I do," said Emily laughing, "and the night that he and the French lady's-maid went out to see the comet—the 'rory-bory alehouse' as he called it—and didn't come in till late, saying they had been frightened by a ghost."

"Well," continued Mr. Tom, "Thady heard through his friends among the gentlemen's gentlemen that a number of male and female servants were to be given admission to the Abbey to wait upon the Peers and Peeresses. So what did the fellow do but imitate his betters, and is buying a place from Lord D.'s valet for a guinea."

We all laughed heartily at this amusing example of high life below stairs.

"Now, Caroline," said Emily to Mrs. Seaforth, "do give us your advice. Both Fanny and I are great readers. Where shall we find the best circulating library? Books we must have, or we shall die."

"Why not try Ebers's shop in Old Bond Street, as you are so near," said Mrs. Seaforth, who was pretty in a languishing sort of way. "It is a pleasant walk from Queen Street. We were going in that direction when we met you. Let us go there together."

The proposal was accepted, and the gentlemen giving us their arms, we were soon at the bookseller's shop. Here we took leave of the Ingoldsby family, engaging ourselves to visit them on the following evening but one.

While Emily spoke with the proprietor, I amused myself by glancing round the shop and examining the newest books. Novels by dear Mr. Dickens, Captain Marryat, Mr. G.P.R. James, Bulwer, Mrs. Gore, Mrs. Trollope, Miss Landon, and all the best writers stood on the shelves or lay about on tables. A life of the Wizard of the North attracted my notice, as did various magazines and books of verse. The Keepsakes and the Annuals presented a charming appearance, and I was interested to see the great historian Gibbon's work on the Roman Empire made suitable for family reading by that Mr. Bowdler who has brought Shakespeare into repute again.

I was placing an order for several new books with an assistant, when a man entered the shop with a large parcel which he placed on the counter.

"Now here, madam," said the assistant, "is a book, a fresh impression newly arrived from the printer's, which you should certainly have; *Jocelyn FitzFulke,* by DeLacy Vavasour. His novels always sell very well. When his last book, *Clarinda Dashbourne, or The Female Orphan's Revenge,* came out, I assure you we had such a crowd that Bond Street was quite blocked. Shall I have the pleasure of putting this up with your other books?"

I refused his offer civilly. Had not Mr. Vavasour promised to send me copies of his works himself? And I confided in his honour.

Emily having transacted our business, and the books having been promised by the same day, I asked that the account for my books might be sent to my father. He might storm, but he could not very well refuse to pay it, and in any case he throws all bills into the fire. When we got home I found a large parcel waiting for me. With trembling fingers I undid it. It contained a complete set of Mr. Vavasour's novels. Enclosed was a gilt-edged card bearing the following inscription, which still brings a blush of pleasurable confusion to the matron's cheek.

Oh, turn away those fawnlike eyes, and close the jalousie!
Thou canst not know how deep thou wound'st the heart till
    now so free.
The VAVASOUR, who in the fight was first among the brave,
Is now in silken fetters bound, FRANCESCA's hapless slave.

This composition caused me acute emotion. Except that my name is not Francesca, nor indeed Fanny either, I having been christened Charlotte at my mother's wish, but my father having had a whim to call me Fanny after a favourite pointer, a name that has clung to me, though this, of course, Mr. Vavasour could not be expected to know, the whole allusion to my appearance at the window seemed to me in the most romantic and poetic taste. I was torn between a desire to show Emily the stanza, and a fear that she might say something unpleasant about it, so I finally determined to leave it carelessly about. Candour would have been in this case the better course to pursue, but this I did not realize till too late.

Emily and I spent the whole evening and most of the night devouring *Jocelyn FitzFulke*. Still can I feel the wild romantic passion, and can remember every word as if it were yesterday. The scene of the novel was laid in Rome, city of Caesar and Pope, prey of the Goth, yet conquering her conquerors! where a widow lady received lodgers in her palace, relic of former splendours. One evening, when the Angelus was ringing from a thousand convents, a gentleman, handsome though careworn, and his wife, arrived at a late hour. The gentleman, an Englishman by his speech and accent, inspected the rooms, engaged them, and went out, saying he would shortly return. Hardly had he left the house than the widow discovered that the young wife was about to become a mother! She gave birth to a lovely female infant and expired. The husband never returned, so the widow brought up the little girl in the strictest piety, treasuring for her the jewels that her unhappy and nameless mother had worn.

A few years earlier, in London, the young Darcy FitzFulke was tending his young wife on the wretched pallet bed in the garret which was their only home, his cruel father, Lord Fitz-Fulke, having cast him off on his marriage to a lovely maiden of slightly lower rank. Too finely nurtured to work, too proud to beg, Darcy could but watch his wife dying day by day, and mingle his tears with hers. A lovely boy, Jocelyn, played about his dying mother's couch, drawing from her wan lips an occasional smile. That night Jocelyn was doubly an orphan. Maddened by the death from starvation and consumption of his fair young wife, Darcy FitzFulke had sought repose in the rolling waters of the Thames!

The haughty Lord FitzFulke then took Jocelyn to his estate and educated him. When the young man was twenty he was sent to Rome to study law, and here he took rooms in the house of the widow. Jocelyn and Mignonne, which I forgot to say was the name of the child left almost an orphan by the death of her mother and the disappearance of her father, felt the dawnings of love, but neither dared avow them to the other. Ah, Youth! A mysterious being called Il Nero now appeared to Jocelyn, and after taking him to a dark and lonely house, magnificently furnished, among the marshes of the Campagna, let him go again. I must confess I could not quite understand this part, but my head was in a whirl and I wished to get to the end of the volume before Emily could get the next one.

Jocelyn, wooed by the shameless Lucrezia, had his faith to Mignonne so sorely tried that he fled to Paris. Here I must mention that I should have mentioned before that he had some years previously rescued a little orphan girl from the ill treatment of a brutal stepmother. On the journey to Paris a handsome stripling named Luigi attached himself to him and the two friends shared an attic in Paris where Jocelyn pursued his studies in law. I cannot clearly remember how it was, but an Englishman whom he met, and who had loved Lucrezia, somehow came to murder someone, which so horrified Jocelyn that he fell into a brain fever. When he recovered, he found that Luigi had been supporting them both by the fruits of his pencil, love having made him an accomplished artist, for he was no other than the orphan girl whom Jocelyn had befriended. I cannot quite recall the events which follow, but Mignonne goes as companion to an English lady of rank, niece to the Earl of Courtenaye, and here the jewels that she wears betray all, for the Earl is none other than her FATHER, who years ago had, under the name of Alphonzo, wooed and won the fair Zulmia, but feared to break the news to his stern father. Thus it was that he left the unhappy Zulmia at the widow's house in Rome, where kindly death following on the pangs of *accouchement* ended her trials. The mysterious being called Il Nero, who had once loved Jocelyn's mother, and hence took so kindly an interest in him, is now poisoned, and the wicked lawyer who, I should have said earlier, had defrauded the widow of all her fortune, thus forcing Mignonne to seek a living as a companion, is justly punished by his son marrying the depraved Lucrezia, thinking that she is a poor but fascinating governess. So Jocelyn, now Earl of Fitz-Fulke, takes Mignonne, now the Lady Flordeliza de Montgomery, to the ancestral home of his grandfather, who has since died of remorse, and the lovers are for ever united.

It was two o'clock in the morning before Emily and I, devouring each volume in turn, had finished the tale. I had the pleasure of reading straight through from the beginning to the end, but Emily had the unfair advantage of knowing what happened at the end before I did, as she began with the third volume, on condition that she would promise not to reveal the *dénouement* to me.

The following day found us languid and heavy, and I altered a head-dress of blonde, adding some green and pink ribbons, while Emily tried a composition of the Polish musician, M. Chopin, on the pianoforte. We both wished that we had been in London during his visit last year, but consoled ourselves with the reflection that we should be able to go to one of the Concerts of Antient Music, or a performance of the Philharmonic Society. Norwich is famous for its music, and I have twice attended a festival there, besides hearing the Oratorio of St. Paul by the German composer Mendelssohn at Birmingham the previous year. I am therefore qualified to judge on questions of musical taste, and I venture to say that Mr. Mendelssohn's works will live. Of M. Chopin's works I cannot so well judge, for Emily has not the brilliance required for their execution. My father had also promised that we should go to Her Majesty's Theatre to see the Italian Opera.

Emily and I discussed at some length the form of a letter of thanks to Mr. Vavasour, but so many copies did we blot or scratch out, that we decided to wait till I could thank him in person. A note from Mrs. Vavasour, requesting us to visit the Exhibition of the Royal Academy in Trafalgar Square with her, slightly roused our drooping spirits, and Emily sewed two feathers into her green hat and placed a small wreath of flowers under the brim. Mrs. Bellows, who had occasion to come into the room, was greatly struck by the improvement effected by this change, so that we ended the day in a more resigned frame of mind.

The day appointed for our visit to the Royal Academy dawned fair and bright and Mrs. Vavasour called for us in her carriage.

"I am sorry," she said as we drove down Piccadilly, "that you did not come to town in time to see Benjamin West's great religious picture of "Christ Rejected" at the Egyptian Hall. There can only be one opinion about a work of art of so elevating a character. My nephew found some fault in the chiaroscuro, but when I gravely pointed out to him that the moral lesson to be drawn from it was of more importance than its artistic merit, great though that is acknowledged to be, he felt the truth of my remark. I hope, my dears, that you will not consider my nephew's company an intrusion at the Royal Academy. DeLacy is the most delightful *cicerone,* and can show you which pictures to admire and which to pass over."

This was indeed good news, and Emily nudged me in a way that caused me to give her a look of rebuke.

Our tour round the galleries was interesting and instructive. Before entering the stately portico Mr. Vavasour pointed out to us the various improvements, the laying out of a regular terrace, the paving of the space beyond it and the fine vista towards Westminster.

"A lover of the picturesque," he said, "may regret the demolition of the houses which formerly stood on this site in romantic disarray, but there are times when the Useful and the Beautiful become One; and such, I consider, has been the case here. Where medieval houses once stood in Gothic confusion, we now have a forum which would not disgrace Ancient Rome; while the King's Stables are replaced by this noble building which houses the art treasures of a nation."

He continued thus to address us as we went into the picture galleries, and presently Mrs. Vavasour, complaining of fatigue, sat down for a while, and Emily remained with her and discussed the fashions, an act of friendship on Emily's part which made my heart sensibly warm to her. I need not say that the picture I was of all most anxious to see was Wilkie's representation of our Young Queen holding her first Council. It was not altogether like his *Blind Fiddler,* engravings of which have deeply affected me, but its effect was most striking. Mr. Vavasour obligingly pointed out to me the principal personages there depicted and told me an amusing story about some person, a Lord Mayor I think, who had got into the Council Chamber under some misapprehension and whose head had been transferred to canvas before he was discovered and removed. Whether the painter subsequently painted out the offending magistrate I do not know.

Another composition which Mr. Vavasour recommended to my judgement was Maclise's *Salvator Rosa painting his friend Masianello,* but as I did not like to expose my ignorance by asking who they were, I preferred to linger on Mr. Landseer's admirable pictures of deer fighting, and Newfoundland dogs, whose expressions are almost human, a quality, as Mr. Vavasour cuttingly remarked, which he denies to his portraits. I find that Mr. Vavasour is a great admirer of Mr. Turner's work, but I confess I preferred Mr. Mulready, whose *Seven Ages of Man* struck me with admiration. Here, indeed, is true imagination! Every detail mentioned by Shakespeare is faithfully rendered, thus constituting a *chef d'œuvre.*

Sir David Wilkie had so far forgotten what is due to the public as to exhibit a portrait of that dreadful O'Connell, who seems to be the cause of most of the unrest in the country. Rather timidly, for one never quite knows what gentlemen's political views are, I asked Mr. Vavasour what he thought of it. His striking answer was:

"The portrait, Miss Harcourt, conveys a very accurate idea of that blustering, burly Hibernian, and is painted with an appropriate coarseness which renders it as disagreeable to look on as the Agitator himself."

Could Mr. Darnley but hear him, he must be convinced that no party which even *dallies* with O'Connell can hope to govern in peace.

When we rejoined Mrs. Vavasour she suggested that if not too fatigued we should also visit the British Institution in Pall Mall.

"I would like," she said, "to have taken you to the Society of Painters in Water-Colours, where Mr. Cattermole is exhibiting his *Scenes from the life of Salvator Rosa,* but we must not attempt too much."

I was relieved to hear this, for I had somehow taken the greatest dislike to this Salvator Rosa, who seemed to meet me at every turn, and I would not like Mr. Vavasour to despise me as an ignorant country girl.

At the British Institution we were greatly struck by Mr. Turner's drawings. Mrs. Vavasour expressed the opinion that Turner is much deteriorated by the introduction of such crude and gaudy colours as he now uses. I saw Mr. Vavasour's lip curl, but with admirable temper he said nothing, merely inviting us all to look at some compositions of Mr. Landseer's. Luckily his aunt was enraptured by them, which restored harmony.

"I must say," she remarked, putting up her glass to examine a picture of some fallow deer, "that the noble bearing and bounding freedom of these beautiful tenants of the forest were never more truly depicted. And do you not think, DeLacy, that in *The Two Dogs* there is a grandeur of composition rarely to be met with in subjects of this description?"

Mr. Vavasour appeared gratified by his aunt's enthusiasm.

Emily, who has not the true gusto for painting, now loudly admired a picture entitled *The Match Boy,* representing a beggar boy offering matches for sale. His pale, emaciated face and ragged garments appeared to me to be faultlessly rendered, but Mr. Vavasour remarked with that air of lofty disdain that sits on him so well:

"The work, Miss Dacre, is indeed well studied and harmoniously coloured, qualities which may well recommend it to you as a work of art; but as a subject, its pauper character and the associations connected with it cannot be regarded as favourable."

"Lassy me!" was all Emily's comment. Emily has no soul.

Mrs. Vavasour left us at our door, asking us to visit her on a day when she would be receiving some literary friends, an invitation which we gladly accepted. She therefore promised to send us cards, and hoped that my father would accompany us.

That evening we passed very pleasantly with the Ingoldsbys, who were at Mivart's Hotel in Grosvenor Square, only a short distance from our lodgings. My father was in an excellent humour because the new gas lighting has not yet been introduced into Grosvenor Square, and he said the oil lamps were like the good old days when he first visited London. Mr. Darnley was also present, and though he has not the romantic appearance, nor the lofty eloquence of Mr. Vavasour, there is something about him which renders intercourse more free and unrestrained. He and Mr. Tom Ingoldsby were discussing the new railways when we arrived. They had both attended the opening of the London and Southampton Railway at Nine Elms, and had been much struck by the faultless and well-sustained pace of the engine, which drew the coaches at the rate of twenty-three miles in forty-five minutes.

"Are you going to the Epsom races by the railway, sir?" asked Mr. Darnley of my father.

"No, sir," answered my father, "I have just bought today a barouche; it is second-hand but has hardly had any use and is in excellent condition. It cost me forty-five guineas and I intend to see the Derby from my own carriage, drawn by my own horses. Have you anything to say against that, sir? Do you think I want to have my hair singed and my face blacked, and let Fanny and Emily here sit next to any impudent Radical fellow that chooses to pay for a ticket?"

He growled several more very uncomplimentary remarks

about Agitators and Radicals, qualifying each with an epithet, but the Ingoldsby family, a delightful goodhumoured set, merely laughed at his vehemence, and Mr. Darnley, who seems determined to find no provocation in anything my father says, changed the subject with a smile.

Mr. Tom Ingoldsby then made us all laugh by producing a bill for the feeding and care of his dog in a livery stable near by. One of the grooms there, being a dog-fancier, had offered to take Mr. Tom Ingoldsby's bulldog under his particular care, and had just sent in his account as follows:

harf pound stick . . . . $2\frac{1}{2}$
harf a gallin best Hail 1.4
Stror for kindle 3
2 pouns stick 10

"I dare say you will be as perplexed as I was," said Mr. Tom. "I made out that stick stood for steak pretty easily, but why the groom should want to kindle straw I couldn't imagine, till it occurred to me that it was his version of the word kennel. As for the best Hail, I am not sure whose throat it went down, his or Growler's."

"Growler is a doat," said Emily. "Do you remember, Tom, the lines you made on him as a puppy? I could quote them yet."

Emily should not speak in a languishing way to young men. It does not become her.

"Fire away," said young Mr. Ingoldsby.

"Now we are in for it," said Mr. Charles Seaforth.

"Oh, Charles, what a vulgar expression!" said Mrs. Seaforth, who, owing to her delicate state of health, was being spectator of rather than participant in our evening's amusement.

"Never mind, Emily, my girl, let us hear Tom's lines," said Mr. Ingoldsby, interrupting a conversation on the Poor Law, on which subject he and my dear father seemed luckily to be in entire concurrence.

Emily, simpering, began.

It was a litter, a litter of five,
Four are drown'd and one left alive,
He was thought worthy alone to survive;
And his master resolved upon bringing him up,
To eat of his bread and drink of his cup,
He was such a dear little cock-tailed pup!

His master taught him many a trick;
He would carry and fetch, and run after a stick,
    Could well understand
    The word of command,
    And appear to doze
    With a crust on his nose
Till his master permissively waved his hand:
Then to throw up and catch it he never would fail,
As he sat up on end on his little cock-tail.

Every one applauded this *jeu d'esprit*, and Emily smiled complacently, as though it were meant for her.

"When will you finish the *magnum opus*, Tom?" asked Mr. Seaforth.

I thought young Mr. Ingoldsby looked a little conscious as he put his brother-in-law's question aside. But now a frightful hubbub arose from the corner where my dear father and Mr. Ingoldsby were talking. Their views on the Corn Law had been more in unison than their views on the Government, and my dear father was driving Mr. Ingoldsby nearly to distraction by his attacks on Lord Melbourne.

"When I think of our young Queen," said my father in a loud and rather talking-at-the-company kind of voice, "being perpetually exposed to the company of a WHIG Prime Minister, a man of doubtful morals, my blood boils. Would you let your

THE FOUR-IN-HAND CLUB AT HYDE PARK CORNEER

THE WATERING-CART THAT SPLASHED EMILY'S DRESS

daughter, Mr. Ingoldsby, spend an hour in the society of such a man?"

"They say he is very charming," said Mrs. Seaforth plaintively, "and then his wife treated him so badly."

"And, of course, being the defendant in a crim. con. case makes him all the more charming in your eyes, ladies," said young Mr. Ingoldsby.

"For my part," said Mrs. Seaforth, "I never can tell which is Mrs. Norton and which Miss Landon. They both write, do they not?"

"My dear madam," exclaimed Mr. Darnley, "how can you say such a thing? Mrs. Norton may have genius—it runs in her family—but she is a woman who has suffered her reputation to become a by-word. Whether guilty or not guilty, she is none the less to be blamed, and is indeed hardly a fit subject for a conversation where ladies are in question. As for Miss Landon, her character is unstained and she has lately married the governor of Cape Coast Castle. There can be no possible comparison between the two."

"Well," said Mrs. Seaforth languidly, "I am sure they will always be exactly the same person to me, but I am no reader."

"If Melbourne was in a crim. con. case, it does but prove what I said," continued my father. "I'd have the fellow shot."

"Like the foxes, sir," said Mr. Darnley laughing.

Young Mr. Ingoldsby, who seems to share with my brother Ned a malicious pleasure in setting his elders on to bait each other, here interposed.

"You should read *Fraser's Magazine,* sir," said he to his father. "There's an excellent poem on the Queen and Lord Melbourne. After comparing her with Queen Anne it runs:

Golden our hopes are, it would fairly dash 'em,
If Mother Melbourne proved your Mother Masham.

"Bravo!" cried my father. "Any man who speaks ill of the Queen should be shot."

"That's enough, Tom," roared Mr. Ingoldsby, and it was some moments before quiet was restored.

I had meanwhile been turning over the pages of the *Monthly Magazine,* and my attention was caught by a poem over the initials L.E.L., which seemed to me so exquisite that I could not but wish to share my pleasure.

"Pray, Mr. Tom," said I to young Mr. Ingoldsby, "do listen to this poem by Miss Landon. I do think it excessively beautiful. It is called *The Zegri Ladye.*"

"And what exactly is a Zegri Ladye?" asked that sarcastic Mr. Tom.

"That's enough, Tom," said Emily, with so just an imitation of old Mr. Ingoldsby's words and tone of a moment ago, that general good humour was restored.

"Indeed, I do not exactly know," said I. "But the sentiment and the language are so affecting that I am sure you will agree with me."

I then read aloud a portion of the poem, but on coming to the lines, which form a kind of refrain,

> Round the purple curtains sweep,
> Heavily their shadows creep
> Around the Zegri Ladye,
> The Ladye weeping there . . .

my sensitive nerves were so much affected that I could not go on. Mr. Darnley, seeing my distress, took the book from me and finished reading the poem with excellent expression. Under cover of the applause which ensued, Mr. Darnley said to me in a low voice:

"Your sensibility, Miss Harcourt, does you honour, and I applaud your taste. Those lines which caused your voice to falter will remain graven in my memory."

I gave him a grateful glance.

Mr. Tom Ingoldsby in his ironical way declared that the Zegri

Ladye was probably frightened of vermin, and that the poem alluded to this fact, and should run

> Round the sable beetles sweep . . .

which caused Mrs. Seaforth to scream.

"Really, Tom, you might have more consideration for your sister," said Mr. Seaforth angrily.

"My dearest Caroline," said young Mr. Ingoldsby going down on his knees, "believe me, 'twas all a jest.

> But Charles must not lodge an ill
> Fear that his progeny'll
> Be like the beetles you find in the kitchen;
> Two twins and three triplets I'm bound he'll be rich in!"

"Get up, dear Tom, and don't be so ridiculous," said Mrs. Seaforth to her brother. "But how Mrs. Norton could write such a poem, about black beetles of all things, I really do not know. No wonder Lord Melbourne did not like her."

A general movement now took place, and after a plan had been made that we should all drive down to the Epsom races, we went back to Queen Street. Mr. Darnley accompanied us to the door, and as he left he pressed my hand, saying:

"May the Zegri Ladye have sweet slumbers."

These words lulled me to sleep.

CHAPTER 5

A DAY AT EPSOM

W hen Emily and I went to Madame Jupon's establishment to have our dresses fitted, we had very little fault to find. I did, indeed, have occasion to call Madame Jupon's attention to a slight misfit in one sleeve, so she spoke with great severity to Miss Smith the assistant, sent her out of the room, and made the alteration herself.

"But," said I, and quite truly, "I would not wish the young woman to get into any kind of trouble on my account."

"You are too kind, madam," said Madame Jupon, "but I am having to discharge her in any case. She has fainted twice in the workroom, which I cannot allow, and if she behaves in that way now, what will it be in three weeks when the dresses are needed for the Coronation? For it is quite settled that it is to take place on the twenty-eighth of June, as you have doubtless heard, and by far the most suitable time, for the dresses which we are now making for it can be worn in July for any further festivities, but if it had been put off till August, my ladies would have had no further use for their new gowns. I am dressing five peeresses for the court balls and the Coronation itself in the Abbey, as well as my usual customers and a few special ladies like yourselves."

We then chose materials for evening dresses, which were to be made with a *corsage à pointe* cut very low and several flounces. Mine was to be in pink crape and Emily's in cream-coloured blonde. Madame Jupon, having all our measurements, promised them within a few days.

On our return we described the dresses to Mrs. Bellows, who takes the greatest interest in our personal belongings. Emily asked her if she would recommend a good but cheap shop where she might purchase stockings as Christmas gifts for the Vicarage servants and her Sunday School children.

"I'm sure I don't know, miss," said Mrs. Bellows. "There did use to be a warehouse in the Poultry kept by Mr. R. Kipling where they had something very cheap in stockings. If I have to go to the City on business, as I sometimes do, would you like me to look in on Mr. Kipling and inquire?"

"Thank you," said Emily, "I should be much obliged. Tell me, Mrs. Bellows, do you think we would do well to wear our new walking dresses, which are to come home this evening, for the races, or should we keep them for a more select occasion?"

"My dear young lady," said Mrs. Bellows, "if you will excuse the liberty, you cannot be young but the once, wherefore, I say, make hay while the sun shines. Wear 'em and tear 'em, as the saying goes, and get your fun while you can. There'll be a plenty of young gentlemen looking at you, I'll be bound."

On the morning of the Epsom races we sustained a slight disappointment. We drove round in the new barouche to Mivart's Hotel, and there found Mr. Ingoldsby with Mr. and Mrs. Seaforth, already seated in their carriage, but neither Mr. Tom Ingoldsby nor Mr. Darnley were to be seen.

"Aha! young ladies!" Mr. Ingoldsby called out as we drove up, "I can see you are looking for Hal Darnley and my Tom. But don't cry your pretty eyes out. They have decided to go by the new railway to Epsom, so off they went to Nine Elms in a hack cab, and are to meet us on the course."

We then set out for Epsom, much regretting the absence of Mr. Darnley, who would have been able to point out the sights to us. Several officers were on horseback in front of the barracks at Knightsbridge, who cast most impudent glances at Emily and myself. When we had passed through Kensington, trying in vain to guess which was the house where Lady Blessington and Count D'Orsay have their literary conversaziones, there was little more of interest to observe. My father slept most of the time, and our chief amusement was to wave at the Ingoldsbys as they overtook us or were overtaken.

When we arrived at the course, our two barouches were drawn up side by side, the coachmen took the horses out, and the footmen unpacked the luncheon we had brought. Under the enlivening influence of champagne my father and old Mr. Ingoldsby became warmly affectionate, and united in drinking destruction to O'Connell and all rick-burners and poachers.

"Mind you," said Mr. Ingoldsby, "I am a Whig, but I'm all for Church and State, and I'll take nothing against the Whigs from any man alive, but I'd no more think of being a Radical than I'd think of moving from Brooks's to the Reform Club. That's all very well for these young fellows like Hal, but they'll come round as they get older."

"Brooks's is a good club," said my father gravely, "but there's too much gaming there. Now at White's we are as steady a set of fellows as you would wish to see."

They then drank to each other's clubs, so Mr. Seaforth suggested that the ladies should take a stroll with him and leave the elders to enjoy themselves in their own way. Accordingly, with Matthews the footman behind us, Emily and I accompanied Mr. and Mrs. Seaforth on a tour of the grounds. Emily, who had been to Epsom on previous occasions was inclined to be a little *ennuyée* and superior, but Mrs. Seaforth and I were in ecstasies at all we saw. The press of vehicles was incredible. Omnibuses, hackney coaches, phaetons, stage coaches, cabs, gigs, carts, chaises, britskas, tilburies, dennets, had been pressed into service for the day. Some of the poorer visitors had come on a kind of flat barrow drawn by a donkey, some looked as if they had walked. On every side were tents for refreshments of all kinds, and booths where showmen and vendors of quack medicines were driving a furious trade. Gipsies in gay attire offered to tell fortunes, but Emily and I did not care to consult them without the protection of a gentleman, and Mr. Seaforth was fully occupied in looking after his wife. It was just at this moment, when both Emily and I were feeling in low spirits, that we beheld Mr. Darnley and young Mr. Ingoldsby.

"Why, Tom," cried Mr. Seaforth, "where have you been this long time?"

"Justifying all the Jeremiads of Miss Harcourt's father against the steam locomotive," said Mr. Tom, laughing, "but that can wait. Hal and I are here, and have found our party, and that is all that matters for the present. Have you laid your money, ladies?"

Mr. Seaforth explained that having three ladies under his care he could not very well do any betting.

"Very right, Charles," said young Mr. Ingoldsby. "I therefore propose that Hal and I should go and do a little business with the bookmakers, after which we will take Emily and Miss Harcourt to the Grand Stand, while you look after Caroline. Ladies, the betting is now about to begin! Have you any favourite?"

I disclaimed any knowledge of the horses, but Emily, with her usual boldness, asked Mr. Ingoldsby to back Lord G. Bentinck's Grey Momus for her.

"Six pairs of gloves if you win," said young Mr. Ingoldsby making off.

"If Miss Harcourt has no objection," said Mr. Darnley to me, "I shall back Amato for us both. The odds are long, but Sir George Heathcote knows a horse, and I love to challenge fortune. The name Amato is one of favourable augury, and with Miss Harcourt as partner, I feel assured that fortune will be on my side."

So saying, he rapidly followed Mr. Tom Ingoldsby, leaving me hardly knowing what to think. When the gentlemen returned they escorted us to the Grand Stand, where we had excellent seats and saw many interesting celebrities, including

Madame Grisi, the opera singer, Taglioni, the famous dancer, and the celebrated Count D'Orsay.

"Do you see that dark-looking foreigner with the Grisi?" asked Mr. Tom Ingoldsby. "That is her husband, de Melcy. Some say he is a count, some say he isn't. They say Lord Castlereagh is sweet on the lady and that de Melcy is only waiting an opportunity to challenge him, but the lady is prudence and virtue itself. Now, Emily, the great race is going to begin. Shut your mouth and use your eyes."

Mr. Darnley kindly lent me an excellent pair of glasses, by the means of which I was enabled to see the noble equines ranged up to start. They seemed very unequal to the occasion, rearing, pawing, going backwards instead of forwards, and exhibiting as much nervousness as if they were human. At last after several false starts they were fairly off, but such was my excitement, that from that moment I saw nothing but flashes of brown or black as they sped past. Emily shrieked several times in a subdued way, and I so far forgot myself as to lay my hand on Mr. Darnley's arm and say:

"Oh, Mr. Darnley, how I hope our horse will win."

Suffice it to say that the gallant bay did win at thirty to one, and his portrait with his jockey Chapple was later painted by the celebrated equine artist Herring. Grey Momus was third.

"The gloves are yours, Miss Harcourt," said Mr. Darnley as we returned to our seats in the barouche.

"Pray, pray," said I, in some confusion, "I was not aware that there was any such arrangement. For Emily to take gloves from Mr. Tom Ingoldsby is quite proper, for they have been friends from childhood, but for me——"

"You are right, Miss Harcourt," returned Mr. Darnley after a moment's silence, "and I applaud your nice feeling of propriety. But do not think that you can so escape the consequences of our bet," added he smiling.

I was at a loss for his meaning, but did not pursue the subject. We found my father and old Mr. Ingoldsby in excellent spirits, as both had backed Amato, and, with a little squeezing, room was found in our barouche for the whole party. Further supplies of champagne enlivened us, and Mr. Ingoldsby asked his son how he had enjoyed the steam locomotive.

"Indeed, sir," said Mr. Tom, a little ruefully, "we never so much as got near it. When Hal and I arrived at Nine Elms, the terminus, we found such a crowd at the station that we could barely force our way through. The waiting-room doors were locked and we could only see through the windows the train, standing in the station, crowded with people of all kinds. Every one was pushing and shoving, the women shrieking like Emily here, and the children squalling. The crowd, pushed on from behind, became more and more 'hobstroppylous' as Thady puts it, and at last burst right through the doors, which were carried off their hinges. Men jumped over the counters and stormed the nearest carriages when, to our great amusement, the railway officials coolly detached the already full carriages whose occupants had paid for their places, and they were drawn away, leaving the rioters behind. No one could tell us whether the remaining coaches would start, and Hal and I were just debating whether we should try our luck in them, when we heard a woman caterwauling so loudly that we had to go to her help. She had had her pocket picked by a light-fingered gentleman, and was hanging on to his coat-tails, shrieking for the police. The ruffian turned round and tried to hit her, but Hal gave him such a blow with his stick as tapped his canister."

"Well done, Darnley," exclaimed my father. "It was the right thing to do. I'd have done it myself—the sneaking French scoundrel."

"But I am not aware that the fellow was French, sir," replied Mr. Darnley.

"That's all one," said my father. "I call 'em Frenchies when they act like Frenchies."

"And pray, Tom," said Emily, "what is to tap a canister?"

"Emily, your ignorance is abysmal," was Mr. Tom's reply.

"To tap a canister is to break a sconce, split a nob, crack the knowledge box, make an incision in the upper apartment, damage the figurehead."

All this he reeled off with so droll an air that I could not keep from laughing.

"But how the devil did you get to Epsom?" asked old Mr. Ingoldsby.

"Well, sir," said Mr. Tom, "having seen the pickpocket taken into custody by a policeman and avoided the worthy woman's thanks, we were just going to try to get into one of the remaining carriages, when a notice was posted up 'No more trains today.' We dashed out, got a cab, gave the driver double fare to whip up his horse, got my britska out, and as the roads were by now fairly empty we tooled along at a spanking pace, and here we are."

My father laughed loudly over this description of a railway journey, and drank confusion to the railways, after which he went to sleep.

We were amused by a gipsy woman who came begging to tell our fortunes. To Mrs. Seaforth she promised a fine handsome family, which, I may say, without passing the bounds of delicacy, was not difficult to prophesy. To Mr. Seaforth she said he must stick to his breeches, which remark Mr. Seaforth and his wife apparently found highly diverting. Mr. Tom Ingoldsby received the news that he would be a great writer of lils, a piece of gibberish we did not understand, while Emily was told to beware of the letter T. I must say, that considering how Emily was laughing and—can I use the word of my dearest friend? *flirting*—with Mr. Tom Ingoldsby, calling him Tom at every other word, the gipsy was not making a wild guess.

On hearing Emily's fate, Mr. Tom laid his hand on his heart and sang in the true Cockney tone:

'Twas going of my rounds in the street I first did meet her,
I thought she was a hangel, just kim down from the skies,

upon which Emily, such are the deleterious effects of the juice of the grape when having drunk more than you are used to, *slapped his hand*. I blushed for her inwardly.

Then came my turn. The gipsy, scanning my hand attentively, told me that I should have a great sorrow, followed by a great joy, and must beware of a beautiful woman and a handsome man.

I thought I detected a certain pleasure on Mr. Darnley's face at these words. He then gave the gipsy a shilling and asked her what she could see.

"You will be on the water," said the gipsy, "and you will have an aching heart."

"Come, that's not enough," said Mr. Darnley, "give me something better."

"Another shilling then, pretty gentleman," said she, with the true gipsy whine. Then drawing close to him she said in a low voice, which none but he and I could hear,

"All will be well when the Zegri Ladye weeps."

Mr. Darnley threw some money to her. I blushed deeply and pretended to be occupied in arranging my dress.

"Here, what's this?" asked my father, suddenly waking up. "Gipsies? Send 'em to the treadmill."

The woman darted a glance of malignant hatred at him.

"I have heard of you, fine gentleman, from our brethren in Norfolk," she said. "Wait for four weeks and then remember the gipsy's warning."

She glided away among the crowd and my father, after a few curses and shouting for a policeman, forgot his anger.

"It is useless to call the police, sir," said Mr. Tom. "They are all occupied in chivvying the poor thimble-riggers and three-card men. This is the dullest Derby, begging your pardon, ladies, that I have ever been to. What with all the sharpers and tumblers, and the farmers and country people being swindled and then fighting the swindlers, there used to be plenty of fun. Now there is no freedom—every little pea and thimble man goes in terror of being committed. It is a shame that we may not enjoy ourselves in our own way."

"Don't say Darby, Tom, it should be Derby," said old Mr. Ingoldsby.

"What will you lay on it, sir?" asked Tom.

"I'll lay five guineas, you impudent dog, to teach you not to doubt your elders," said Mr. Ingoldsby laughing.

"Done, sir," said Mr. Tom, writing the bet down in his book.

"What did I say about Brooks's?" cried my father. "You Whigs would lay a bet on your mother's funeral."

The rest of the afternoon was without incident. We left the field before the end of the races, to avoid the crowd, Emily accepting a seat in Mr. Tom's britska, and Mr. Darnley coming with us. Although my father slept most of the way home, Mr. Darnley and I were not able to speak with freedom. The consciousness of the gipsy's mysterious words about the Zegri Ladye was in both our minds.

It was not surprising on our return to find that my maid Upton had gone out, without permission, with Mr. Seaforth's Irish servant, as Mrs. Bellows indignantly informed us, and that the little cockney servant had broken, or so she said, a bottle of port. Mrs. Bellows accused her of having drunk it, my father gave way to temper and swore that one was as badly rooked in London lodgings as in a gambling hell. Shocked by his violence Emily and I went to our room, and when Upton returned I rated her soundly for her impertinent conduct, till she cried and promised not to offend again.

I will not weary my readers with an account of the exact way in which we spent our days. To a country visitor London is an ever-enthralling spectacle, but to the sated town-dweller the gold appears but pinchbeck. Emily, who knew London better than I, took charge of our sight-seeing, and sometimes together, sometimes with Mrs. Vavasour or Mrs. Seaforth, we saw most of the attractions of the metropolis.

Madame Tussaud's Exhibition Bazaar in Baker Street interested me greatly, as we saw there our young Queen and all the Royal family perpetuated in waxen mould. The figures were all lifelike in the extreme, though Mrs. Vavasour, who was with us, assured us that while the figures of strangers appeared to be speaking likenesses, yet any celebrity whom she happened to know was shockingly travestied. The portrait of Madame Tussaud herself struck us very much, and Emily thought she looked horrid.

The Cosmorama in Regent Street was also highly instructive. Here we saw the Ruins of Palmyra, Algiers, the Mer de Glace, and St. Peter's at Rome, so vividly depicted that imagination could persuade herself that she was transported to the very regions in question.

Mrs. Vavasour drove us one day to see the material for the Queen's Coronation robes. It has been woven by a very respectable person named Edward Howe, in Castle Street, Shoreditch, and is indeed rich and rare. My father, who had accompanied us, gave the man a guinea for "beating the Frenchies at their own job," which the man pocketed gladly enough, though I saw him exchange winks with some of the bystanders. Papa is sometimes more than a daughter can endure. Private annoyance is bad enough, but public mortification is unbearable. However, parents are created to distress us, and let me not forget that Emily too has her trials. Never shall I forget her account of the Sunday when her father, usually all that a parent should be, actually sent her home from the very church door for wearing a bonnet which he considered unbecoming to the daughter of a rector of the Church of England. Poor Emily, who had for the moment indulged in a tender sentiment for a handsome young Evangelical preacher whom she had met while at Miss Twinkleton's school at Cloisterham, and who was subsequently imprisoned for abducting an heiress, had taken to wearing plain bonnets as a sign of regeneration. She was forced to go home and put on a bonnet with feathers and ribbons, and from that moment she has never again flirted—again that dreadful word! but some

train of association always produces it when Emily is in question—
with the false and insidious doctrines of the Evangelical school.

It must have been shortly after this visit to Shoreditch that
Emily, on receiving a letter from her father one morning at
breakfast, burst into loud sobs. My father, who was reading *The
Times*, asked what the devil was the matter that a man couldn't
read his paper in peace. Throwing a reproachful look at him, I
went to Emily's assistance, and after administering sal volatile,
she was able to murmur amid sobs the words, "Lieutenant
Bennett."

As the name conveyed nothing to me, I endeavoured to
soothe her and satisfy my curiosity.

"What are the Government coming to?" said my father,
throwing the paper angrily down. "Here's a fine affair at Canterbury. Riots, constables killed, a young officer shot. It's all the
Whigs, damned Frenchified scoundrels. Pitt wouldn't have
stood it, nor would the Duke."

At the words "young officer," Emily cried so loudly that
nature was exhausted, and she had to stop to breathe.

"Now, dearest Emily," said I ringing the bell and telling
Upton to bring several clean handkerchiefs, "confide in me."

"I once danced with Lieutenant Bennett, when the 45th were
stationed at Canterbury," said Emily, her voice almost inaudible
with emotion, "and now he is shot."

"Let me see the account," I cried, seizing *The Times* and
casting my eye over a long article, which I could hardly read for
indignation. It appeared that some low demagogue named
Thom, but newly released from an asylum for the insane, had
preached a kind of crusade in Kent, blasphemously calling
himself sometimes Sir William Courtenay, and sometimes the
Saviour. Under his order some misguided peasants had attempted a rising. Constables had been sent to stop them, one of
whom had been shot and stabbed by Thom. The military had
then been called out, the riots having assumed alarming propor-
tions, and this unfortunate Lieutenant Bennett had been shot

dead by Thom. The soldiers roused to fury by the fall of their officer, had then very properly bayoneted the villain Thom.

Having mastered these details, I returned to my task of consoling Emily, and on questioning her found that though she had once danced with the unfortunate officer at a subscription ball at Canterbury, she had no recollection of his appearance or conversation. This sensibility appears to me to be misplaced. I told her so, and we had a sharp quarrel, during which my father left the room, shutting the door violently behind him.

To calm Emily's spirits I ordered the carriage, and we drove to Howell and James to look at hats, and then to Waterloo House to buy shawls. Thus the Canterbury Riots were effaced from our memory, though I find that even now there are troubles arising from those lamentable disturbances. However, as it is business connected with them that has called Mr. Darnley to Canterbury and so enabled me to read the *Ingoldsby Legends* and undertake the writing of these slight memoirs, all may be for the best.

On the same day I was both gratified and embarrassed to receive from Mr. Darnley a beautifully bound copy of the poems of Miss Landon, in which he had marked the passages he thought most striking. This, he said laughingly, was in payment of his sporting debts, "for," he added, "without my happy association with Miss Harcourt, fortune would not have smiled on me as she did. By the way, Miss Harcourt," he added, "you may be interested to hear that our friend old Mr. Ingoldsby has won his five guineas. He wrote to the Editor of *Bell's Life* and has had the following answer in the Correspondent's column; 'It is Derby, not Derby in pronunciation.' Tom paid up handsomely, but maintains that Darby is correct and that he will stick to it."

He then handed a packet to Emily which he said was from Mr. Tom Ingoldsby. Emily opened it and found six pairs of French gloves, and written on a card, "Beware the letter T," at which she had the grace to look quite confused.

CHAPTER 6

LITERARY LIONS AND ETON MONTEM

We were now gratified to receive cards from Mrs. Vavasour for one of her evenings. I feared I would have some difficulty in persuading my father to come with us, as he said he preferred a snug evening at White's, and had it not been for a lucky accident, Emily and I would have been obliged to go alone. My father had, at his club, come across a book about hunting, by a Mr. Jorrocks I think, though I believe that was not his name. To this book he had taken one of his violent fancies, and quoted from it in season and out of season, mostly, I must admit, out of season, sometimes mortifying me excessively by the very malapropos remarks which must have made people think him a strange kind of country character. Happening to allude to this book in the presence of Mr. Vavasour, my father expressed a desire to meet the author and shake his hand.

Mr. Vavasour, a kind of shudder running over his expressive features, politely replied:

"If the author can be found, sir, I will engage that my aunt will have him at one of her lionizing evenings, and will have much pleasure in introducing him to you."

At this promise my father was delighted, and on the appointed evening was ready full half an hour before the time. On arriving at Mrs. Vavasour's house in St. James's Place we were shown into a very elegant saloon, brilliantly lighted. Mrs. Vavasour came forward to meet us, expressing her particular pleasure at seeing my father.

"Our lions have not yet arrived, sir," said Mr. DeLacy Vavasour, as he bowed to our party, "and my aunt exceedingly regrets that the author of Mr. Jorrocks cannot be found."

My father's answer, which I really do not like to put upon paper, was, "Blister my kidneys!"

"Lassy me!" cried Emily, "what will Mrs. Vavasour think, Mr. Harcourt? That is one of your Mr. Jorrock's sayings, is it not? Lord, I never could read such a book."

A slight stir now took place as the name of Lady Almeria Norbourne was announced and our hostees and her hephew went forward to welcome the new-comer. I can even now see her as she entered the room. Of middle height, but exquisitely proportioned, the Lady Almeria had a face of pure oval form. Her high white brow was shaded by hair of rich chestnut, falling in glossy curls upon her alabaster shoulders, and lightly confined by a fillet with a jewelled clasp. Her delicately pencilled eyebrows were arched over large eyes of deepest cerulean blue. Her nose was pure in outline as though chiselled by the hand of Gibson. Her lips, of the deepest vermilion, were full and imperious, and could yet bend to an *espiègle* archness. Her rounded figure was moulded by a dress of pure white silk from the richest looms of Cashmere, while a scarf of finest gauze half hid, half revealed a bust which might have served a Canova as model. She wore no ornaments except a necklace of cameos richly set with diamonds, and her arms were clasped with maginificent bracelets. As she seated hereself I had a glimpse of a fine white stocking and elegant black shoes which might have been Titania's own.

My heart sank as I looked on her. Jealousy I could not feel for one whom I could not hope to emulate, but how deeply did I wish that I were an earl's daughter with a fortune. Why I know not, I suddenly felt very angry with Mr. Vavasour, and when he came back to us and inquired after my health, I merely gave him

a civil reply and walked away. Mrs. Vavasour then presented me
to Lady Almeria, whose conversation was, I will not say vapid,
but showed no evidence of deep thought, though her beauty was
even more dazzling on a closer inspection than at a distance. I
then saw Mr. Darnley enter the room. He approched and seated
himself by us, being apparently known to Lady Almeria, for her
ladyship roused herself from her state of abstraction and entered into an animated conversation about people, mostly of
title, unknown to me. I sat rather silent and low, deeply conscious of how inferior I must appear in Mr. Darnley's eyes,
though he, with real kindness, did his best to draw me into the
conversation. At length the talk turned on books, and Lady
Almeria inquired of Mr. Darnley whether he had read *The
Sorrows of Rosalie.*

"Indeed, Darnley," said her ladyship, arranging her bracelets,
"you should read it. The verse is quite melting. All about love
and poor forsaken women, you know; but then you men are such
deceivers. I positively wept over it. You have such feeling you
would doat on it."

"I must certainly follow your advice," said Mr. Darnley. "Who
is the author?"

But before Lady Almeria could answer, Mrs. Vavasour brought
up a gentleman to be presented to her, and Mr. Darnley, rising,
offered me his arm to move to another part of the saloon.

"These parties are hardly in my line," he said, "but hearing
from Vavasour, whom I know slightly, that Mr. and Miss
Harcourt were to be here, I called upon Mrs. Vavasour and
obtained an invitation."

The company was not numerous, but highly select, and the
conversation was mostly of a literary turn. The subject of Annuals was mentioned, and Mr. Vavasour was very satirical about
them.

"The sight of a table covered with tabbyfied Annuals," said
he, "is to me more nauseating than an apothecary's shop. My
aunt cannot altogether resist them, but I have succeeded in

making her confine her purchases to the *Gems of Beauty* and the *Keepsake*. They are really the only tolerable ones, though that is not saying much."

"At least, DeLacy," said his aunt, "even your fastidious taste cannot find fault with the *Gems of Beauty*. Parris's admirable designs of the Twelve Passions, each a refined type of feminine beauty, and Lady Blessington's delightful poems on the same subjects, are a treat for the connoisseur."

"Come, DeLacy, you must admit that the *Keepsake* this year is really full of feeling," said Lady Almeria. "I hardly slept a wink after reading *The Vampire Knight and his Cloud Steed*, and the story of *Sophie of Hanover and Mimi the Faithful Waiting Maid* is so historical as well as so melting. But I dare say," she added archly, "that as an author you are jealous."

"I do not attempt to compete with our poetesses," said Mr. Vavasour. "I might even say that it would be impossible. Who, for instance, could emulate the style of your friend Lady Emmeline Stuart Wortley?"

"Oh, her *Lays of Leisure Hours,*" said Lady Almeria. "They are quite superlative. Who could be so insensible as not to feel their merit?"

"Let us allow the company to judge," said Mr. Darnley, picking up a book that lay on a table by him. "Here is the work in question. I will open at random and read."

We all composed ourselves to listen and Mr. Darnley read aloud as follows:

> *The Dragon Fly*
> The Dragon Fly
> Shoots spooming by,
> No shape is seen
> Except between
> Those whirlwind-flights
> Whose quickness smites
> The sense with pain—

It leaves a train
Of pompous hues
That do suffuse
The chrystal air
With kindlings rare . . .

"There are one hundred and thirty pages of this poem," said Mr. Darnley coolly, as he turned over the leaves, "so I will only read one more stanza:

Oh! Dragon Fly,
When thou dost die,
Depart from thee
All things that be."

No one seemed quite to know how to take this.

"But, Mr. Darneley," said I, "surely Mr. Dickens must have read that poem, for does not the last stanza bear a striking resemblance to Mrs. Leo Hunter's *Ode to an Expiring Frog?*"

"Oh, Dickens," said Lady Almeria, "he is low, decidedly low. Besides Lady Emmeline's poems are newly out, so he could not have seen them."

"In that case," said Mr. Darnley gravely, "her ladyship must have copied Mr. Dickens. There is such a thing as Nature copying Art."

Several of the company laughed at this cutting remark, but I thought Lady Almeria looked offended.

"Quite right to stand up for Boz, Darnley," said my father. "Pickwick made me laugh, I can tell you. Capital fun all that about Mr. Winkle trying to ride and shoot. As for all this namby-pamby, milk-and-water poetry, it's quite above my head. Leave that to the Frenchies. Come, Fan, it's time we were jogging."

"But, Papa," cried I in alarm, "the evening has scarcely begun, we cannot be so rude as to leave."

"Indeed, Mr. Harcourt, you must not think of leaving us so

soon," said Mrs. Vavasour. "A young friend of ours, the Member for Maidstone, has just arrived, and has expressed a wish to meet such a representative of the English country gentleman as Mr. Harcourt. You cannot refuse."

With an ill grace my father submitted to being led away.

"Observe my aunt's friend," said Mr. Vavasour to me. "Disraeli is his name, doubtless familiar to you through his father's writings. Disraeli himself has written several brilliant if ephemeral novels, which is all very well for us poor scribblers, but hardly quite the thing for a serious politician. But I daresay he will give up Parliament, as there were some unpleasant passages over his election. Though he is Jew there is something uncommonly fascinating about him, and you never know what he is really thinking."

My father now reappeared in the company of a young man of striking person. He had a somewhat foreign air, with long black ringlets and dark eyes. He was remarkable for the brilliance of his costume and the number of chains, watches, and rings that he wore, but his address was easy—almost too easy I thought.

"I am delighted to have the honour of meeting Miss Harcourt," he said, "and it is gratifying, though not surprising, to find so fair a flower grafted upon so fine and rugged a trunk. England is full of these anomalies; it is a part of her charm. In your father, Miss Harcourt, I find my ideal of the good old English squire. I can see his household in my mind's eye. He dispenses justice, protects and cultivates the affection of a grateful and dependent peasantry, and exercises the open-handed hospitality which is our country's pride, at a table where the wines of sunny Gascony mingle in harmony with dishes that might whet the jaded appetite of the epicure."

My father, who had been listening with considerable astonishment to this portrait of his domestic life, here burst out:

"Damn all French wines and French kickshaws, I say. Roast beef and ale was good enough for my father and it's good enough for me. I'll drink a bottle of port, or four or five for that matter, with any man, for the Portygees are old friends of ours. But as for your French vinegar, it gives a man the colic."

Mr. Disraeli appeared not a whit abashed by this outburst, and indeed eyed my father with a species of approval as he continued:

"Mrs. Harcourt, sir, is doubtless equally a queen in her own domain of jellies and elderflower water, tends the needy poor, and by teaching the children of a robust yeomanry the elements of the Christian faith, sheds universal benevolence."

"I'll be d—d if she does," said my father. "We have a house-keeper to make the jellies and a parson to teach the children their catechism, and if they don't that's their lookout. I don't hold with all this meddling. Damn all Bible Societies!"

Of course, as might have been foreseen, my dear father had been partaking liberally of the refreshments that were in an adjoining room. Much mortified I wentin search of Mrs. Vava-sour, who with genuine kidness assured me that she was not in the least offended.

"My own father was rarely in a state to appear after dinner," said she, "and though it is no longer fashionable, I know Mr. Harcourt is a follower of the old ways, and I can make every allowance. Dear Fanny, pray do not distress yourself. Mr. Dis-raeli has a great admiration for character, and will take a lively interest in your father's prejudices. Forget this incident."

So speaking she led me to another room where I found Emily with a party of younger people of both sexes. Here I spent an hour very pleasantly, at the end of which time my father came up, now in high good humour, to bid us make our adieus.

"Good-bye, young man," said he, wringing Mr. Disraeli's hand, "you're a rum 'un, but you're a deep 'un."

Mr. Disraeli looked flattered at these words, and replied that he was delighted at Mr. Harcourt's approbation, and at the similarity of their opinions about the Radicals.

"Radicals? Damned French smugglers, I call 'em," said my father. "Come on, girls."

As we bade farewell to our hostess I heard Mr. Vavasour say to Mr. Disraeli:

"Nature copying art again, my dear fellow. Were you not flattered to meet a character from *Vivian Grey* in the flesh?"

"Oh, Sir Christopher Mowbray," said Mr. Disraeli laughing. "But talking of books, I have not yet had time to read *Jocelyn Fitz-Fulke,* but I hear on all hands that it is to be the success of the season. I shall hear your name so praised at Gore House, to which I am now on my way, that I shall perish of envy."

"The author of *Henrietta Temple* need not feel envy of any man alive," said Mr. Vavasour.

"Ah, my dear Vavasour, you flatter me. Your works will be read when mine are forgotten," said Mr. Disraeli with a smile that made me think of Mr. Vavaour's saying that one never knew what he was thinking.

"And when will you next delight us by some product of your pen?" asked Mr. Vavasour.

"Who knows? Writing is a bore. Politics are a bore. I may go to the East again. Farewell, my dear fellow."

Lady Almeria, in an exquisite pink wrap trimmed with swans-down was standing in the hall.

"I wish I could take you on to Almack's, Darnley," said she, "I am just on my way there with the Marchioness of E. It is a monstrous shame that you are not on the list. I must positively see to it that your name is included. And, Darnley, do not forget to read *The Sorrows of Rosalie.*"

"I shall remember your recommendation," said Mr. Darnley. "You were about to tell me the author's name when we were interrupted upstairs."

"Mrs. Norton. You must meet her, Darnley. She is quite a protégée of mine."

"I am surprised, your ladyship," said Mr. Darnley in a serious tone, "that you should know Mrs. Norton. *She does not live with her husband.*"

I should have thought that the gravity of this rebuke would have abashed her, but she replied:

"Lord! Of course she doesn't. How could she after that crim. con. affair? Besides, he is so stingy. He has actually put a notice in the papers to say he will not pay her debts. She is already in debt for her carriage and horses, and you know, Darnley, one cannot go through a season without an equipage. The man from whom she hires is suing Norton for the amount and I hope he will get it. I certainly would not live with Norton were he *my* husband. But I must be gone. You know the magic doors of Almack's close at midnight, and my chaperone is waiting."

So saying she glided from the hall and entered her carriage.

"Good God!" exclaimed Mr. Darnley, as if to himself. "How can one so lovely be so lost to all delicacy!"

I was very sorry that Mr. Darnley was so deeply affected, though I could not but be glad that his opinion of Lady Almeria had been lowered, and I determined for the future to think all the ill I could of Mrs. Norton.

My father wished to finish the evening at White's, but Mr. Darnley, for whom my father had taken a great liking, assisted us to persuade him to go home. Mr. Darnely told me privately that he heard my father had been gambling heavily at White's, so an evening which had begun with pleasurable anticipation ended with gloomy presentiments.

Tuesday the fifth of June was Whitsun Tuesday, the day of the Eton Montem. I had previously attended this ceremony three years ago, when my brother William was in the Lower School, but Emily had never seen it, so my father and I were to drive with her to Eton, Mr. Tom Ingoldsby, formerly a scion of that illustrious seat of learning and the birch, being also of our party. William was now in the Sixth Form and to leave school at the end of the half, and he was to be one of the salt-bearers. Indeed I had forgotten to say that he had written to my father asking for twenty guineas to get a fancy dress, upon which my father had very injudiciously sent him thirty. We shall see later to what purpose William had been putting this munificence.

On the journey Emily inquired of my father what Montem exactly was. ~

"Montem? Why, we always went Ad Montem," said my father. "I was dressed as a Wallachian, it was in Dr. Davies's time, with red leather boots and a scarlet sash and a helmet and a great wig, and a fine sight I must have looked. Old Davies, that was our headmaster then, you know, was a fine old fellow, but he quarrelled with the masters and couldn't manage the boys. We had a fine riot, I remember, and pelted him out of Upper School with books and ink-pots and anything we could lay hands on. But he made it up with the masters, and we had to stand to attention again."

"But you were to tell Emily about Montem, sir," said Mr. Tom Ingoldsby.

"Quite right; where was I? Well, d'ye see, the day after Montem the older boys used to wear their Montem coats, a kind of custom among us, so the Doctor flogged us all. So we got his cat and stole one of his wigs and tied it on to his cat's head. Lord, how it squalled and scratched till we cut its claws, and then we fastened squibs to its tail and let it loose in the School Yard, and though the Doctor flogged the whole form, no one gave the joke away."

"I take it, sir," said Mr. Tom Ingoldsby, "that the floggings made a man of you."

"By Gad, young man, you are right," said my father, "they did. And if I was a boy I'd say the same again."

Mr. Tom gave Emily and me a most comical look.

"But pray," said Emily, "what is Montem?"

"The first provost of Eton was a monk, who sold his soul to the devil on condition that his black majesty would build the college in a night," said Mr. Tom, "and every three years the boys have to wave a flag and go in a procession, or the school will all disappear in a clap of thunder and the devil will fly away with the present provost. It is called Ad Montem by a piece of what is called euphemism, that is they go up a hill in honour of the devil, to avoid mentioning the place below."

"No, Mr. Tom," said I, "you shall not so tease poor Emily. Montem, my dear Emily, is a ceremony which takes place every three years, its origin being lost in the mists of antiquity. It commences by a number of boys, of whom William will be one, in fancy dress, taking their places on the roads round Windsor and Eton. They collect money which they call "salt," and this money is given to the Captain of Montem to enable him to proceed to King's College and there continue his education. Then there is a fine procession to Salt Hill and the standard bearer waves the flag, and after that they all dine at the inns, and are very merry. Last Montem William was in the Lower School and was only a poleman. He wore a blue jacket and white trousers and carried a long white wand, which other boys with swords had to try to cut in two, I do not know why, but it was all very delightful."

"Admirably described, Miss Harcourt," said Mr. Tom. "May I add for Miss Dacre's benefit that the unfortunate Captain has to defray all expenses for the day, besides making good any damage that the boys have done, so that he rarely gets more than a small part of the money collected."

As we drew near Eton four carriages passed us at a rapid pace and we heard shouts of "The Queen." Just as we came to the bridge two boys stopped the carriages, demanding "Salt." Our barouche drew up just behind the last carriage, in which was seated the Queen herself! Emily and I clutched each other, Mr. Tom stood up and bowed, while my father, waving his hat in the air, shouted: "God bless your Majesty and down with the French!"

Her Majesty looked smilingly in our direction and graciously bowed. One of her attendants gave a purse to the saltbearer, who then approached our carriage. What was my joy to perceive that it was William! He was richly and tastefully attired as a Cavalier, in a plum-coloured suit trimmed with blue lace. He wore high

ETON MONTEM

HER

MAJESTYs 👑 THEATRE

ITALIAN OPERA HOUSE.

THIS EVENING,
TUESDAY, April 9, 1839,

Will be performed, BELLINI'S celebrated Opera

I Puritani.

Lord Walter Walton (Governor General) Sig. MORELLI
Sir George (his Brother) Sig. LABLACHE,
Lord Arthur Talbot (a Partizan of the Stuarts) Sig. RUBINI
Sir Richard Forth (a Colonel) Sig. TAMBURINI,
Sir Bruno Robertson, [an Officer] Sig. G. GALLI,
Henrietta of France (Widow of Charles I.) Made. CASTELLI
Elvira (Daughter of Lord Walton) Made. GRISI

After which, will be produced, an entirely

NEW BALLET, IN TWO ACTS,

By Signor GUERRA, on the subject, and the Music selected from MAYERBEER'S

ROBERT LE DIABLE

Principal Dancers:

Mademoiselle H. ELSLER,
Mademoiselle BELLON,

Madame CARE   Madame GIUBILEI,
Mademoiselle PIERSON,   Mademoiselle BRIESTROPP,

Signor GUERRA,
M. GOSSELIN,   and   M. MATHIEU

Mr. LAPORTE has the honor to inform the Subscribers and the Public that, in order to afford additional Strength and Power to the Company, he has engaged the popular *Italian Tenor* from the Opera in Paris,

Signor MARIO,

Whose First Appearance will take place next Month.

The necessary arrangements for the better accommodation of the Visitors to the Pit and Gallery of this Theatre, making it imperative that **NO ORDERS** should be issued, Mr. LAPORTE begs to inform his Friends, that no application for Orders or Gratuitous admission, can in future be attended to.

☞ Just imported, a large quantity of OPERA GLASSES, which are on sale or hire at Mr. SALOMON's, 67, Haymarket, three Doors from Charles Street.

Doors open at half-past 7, begin at 8 o'clock, precisely.

PIT, 10s, 6d.   UPPER STALLS, 5s.   GALLERY, 3s.

Application for Boxes, Stalls, and Tickets to be made at the Box Office of the Theatre.

George Stuart, Printer, 15, Archer Street, Haymarket.

PROGRAMME OF THE OPERA

leather boots, a large hat with drooping plumes, and a handsome wig with long curls.

"Dearest William," I cried, "how you have grown! How
handsome you look in your dress!"

"I say," said William, taking no notice of my greeting except
by a scowl, "can't some one tell the governor not to make a show
of himself? I shall be finely roasted by the fellows for having a
father who shouts Down with the French."

"Well, William my boy," said my father, who luckily had not
heard these unfilial words, "you look mighty fine. What are you
eh? Not a Frenchy, I hope?"

"No sir," said William. "I am one of Charles I's noblemen."

"Quite right," said my father, "Always support the Throne.
How is everything, William? No floggings, eh?"

William looked extremely sulky, but replied as civilly as is
possible when a parent exasperates one to the verge of frenzy,
"Nothing to speak of, sir. I hope you are ready with your salt.
Her Majesty has given us a hundred pounds."

My father put ten guineas into the silk bag and William,
raising his plumed hat, walked quickly away, not, however,
before he had given Papa the ticket which frees all who have
paid their salt from further importunities.

On our arrival we proceeded to the Great Quadrangle to see
the procession of the boys, which is a pretty sight. While the flag
was being waved we caught a glimpse of the Queen at a window
in the Provost's house. She appeared to be smiling, and delighted with everything she saw. We then drove as near to Salt
Hill as possible and had some luncheon in the carriage, after
which a loud cheering announced the arrival of Her Majesty,
whose carriage was driven up to the foot of Salt Hill. The lady
sitting next to her was, we gathered, the Duchess of Kent, and a
lady-in-waiting sat opposite them. The long procession as-
cended the hill, where the flag was again waved, while the crowd
loudly applauded. The fancy dresses were truly superb. Here we
saw a Grecian warrior of antiquity, there a voluptuous turbaned

Ottoman. A Highland Chief in full martial garb jostled a Spanish Hidalgo; a Crusader talked with an Albanian in crimson and gold with snowy tunic. The Sixth and Fifth Form boys, except those acting as salt bearers, were in their usual millitary uniform, some in red coats, some in blue, with cocked hats and feathers, while the pages attending them were in rich medieval attire.

William, his duties being now over, came up to us.

"Well, Emily," said he, "how did you like it all?"

"I never saw anything so fine," said Emily. "And such crowds, and the cheering!"

"We'll have far more crowd next Montem unless old Hawtrey and the Provost can stop the railways," said William. "Why, several train loads came down to Slough yesterday, when the new line from the Paddington Station to Maidenhead was opened, and there will be many more today."

At the word railway my father, who was dozing, woke up.

"What's that? A railway at Eton?" he ejaculated.

"No, sir, hardly as bad as that," said William laughing, "but there is a sort of station at Slough. Dr. Goodall, the Provost, is half mad about it, and says the fellows will be off to town without permission, and he and Hawtrey are determined to fight the railway companies tooth and nail."

"Quite right too," said my father, now thoroughly roused by the mention of the hated locomotives. "We never had a railway at Eton in my time. Dr. Davies would have seen to that. If I had my way I'd deliver all the railway contractors to Dr. Keate to be flogged. Damned smuggling Frenchmen!"

"Have you been in the railway, sir?" asked William of Mr. Tom.

Mr. Tom then obligingly gave William an account of his experiences on the London and Southampton Railway, and his difficulties in getting to Epsom. A Lower School boy who had come up with some message for William stood listening open-mouthed. When Mr. Tom had finished, the boy gave a long whistle.

"By Jove," said he, "I'll be an engine-driver when I leave school! I say, Harcourt, you are wanted at the Christopher."

"Good-bye then, Fanny and Emily," said William. "I am very grateful for the money you gave me for my dress, sir. I suppose you haven't any more of the ready about you?"

I really thought my father would explode, so taken aback was he by the Lower Boy's monstrous choice of a profession and William's cool demand. However, he recovered himself sufficiently to let loose a volley of hearty oaths, which were doubtless treasured by the Lower School boy, after which he gave William five guineas and a guinea to the little boy, who went into transports of joy and rushed off crying "Sock, sock!"

"He will spend it all on toffy," said William. "This kind gift of yours, sir, will save your unworthy son's honour, as I got confoundedly into debt over the Derby. By the way, sir, I hope you are going to give me a good sum for Leaving Money. Old Hawtrey pretends he don't notice what you give, but that don't prevent his taking it."

Without waiting for a reply he was off, and my father told the coachman to drive home. He was in a state of red-hot heat about railways, boys, and the degeneracy of modern times, but Mr. Tom, by his unfailing good humour and his jokes and puns, succeeded in making him unbend, and the journey home was very pleasant. As Mr. Tom said, it is comforting to see the regular observance of our old English institutions, and this custom of Montem is at least one which has stood the test of time and will continue to be observed while Eton flourishes!

CHAPTER 7

LEANDER *versus* CAMBRIDGE

My brother Ned came down from Cambridge about a week before the rowing match, but did not stay with us, because he had to be in training with the others of his crew. Mr. Darnley was similarly occupied, so we saw very little of him. I noticed, however, that Ned inquired most particularly of me what Emily's engagements were, and if she were at home it was almost a matter of course that Ned should visit us. Emily appeared to take the greatest interest in his accounts of his dog, the gig he drives at Cambridge, his play at billiards, his racing bets, his rowing exploits, and all the subjects which a sister's partiality finds so excessively boring. I also observed that Emily had a liveliness, verging at times on forwardness, when Ned was present, and a languor when he was absent, upon which I placed an interpretation very favourable to Ned's advances. Knowing how annoying the presence of a relation can be in our tenderer moments, and remembering well how very trying my dear father used to be when Colonel Sparker rode over from Norwich to see me, always coming into the room to ask the Colonel to look at a gun or a dog, as if there were nothing else worth looking at, I took care to leave the two *soupirants* alone, while in the seclusion of my bedroom I devoured the literature supplied by the library. I remember that about this time I read *The Vicar of Wrexhill* by Mrs. Trollope, and thought highly of it. The character of the sanctimonious Evangelical parson, Mr. Cartwright, is excellently drawn, and I shuddered at the way in which he enmeshes the unhappy and foolish widow in his toils till he persuades her to give him her hand and fortune. It is a striking representation of the way in which a false religion can alienate even a mother from her children. The sufferings of Charles and Helen as they see their mother becoming a prey to the designing Cartwright, and find her affection subtly withdrawn from them and given to persons with whom she would once have been too fastidious to associate, are almost unbearable. How I rejoiced when, after the poor mother's death, the villain is foiled and virtue triumphs, and the Anglican persuasion reigns once more.

One evening I mentioned the subject of religion to Mr. Vavasour.

"Nature is my religion, Miss Harcourt," he said, "but that does not prevent me from recognizing other forms. For instance, I would readily dine with the Archbishop of Canterbury, as indeed I am to do tomorrow. Living in society, one should live sociably."

"Do not listen to him, Miss Harcourt," said Mr. Tom Ingoldsby, for this conversation took place at a concert of the Royal Philharmonic Society at the Hanover Square Rooms, which Emily and I were attending in company with the two gentlemen. The Sinfonia in B flat by Beethoven had just ended amid applause, and at last we could talk. "He is attempting to impose on your ignorance. Any one, you must know, can go to the public dinners at Lambeth, if he is in society and puts his name down beforehand in a book provided for the purpose. I am willing to lay a guinea that Dr. Howley has not the pleasure of Vavasour's acquaintance."

"Hooley, my dear fellow, Hooley," said Mr. Vavasour.

"Howley or Hooley, you will not take my challenge," said Mr. Tom laughing. "I believe Howley, like you, was a sad Radical in his younger days and used to have a portrait of Tom Paine over his mantelpiece; but now we must be silent, for the next item is beginning, and we should listen to Cinti Damoreau. She is singing something of Rossini's."

"Oh, I think Rossini is a doat," cried Emily, and was hushed by the listeners around her.

The orchestra was under the direction of Mr. Moscheles, and I was prepared to find it in the first flight of taste, but both Mr. Vavasour and Mr. Tom Ingoldsby, who have pretensions to be connoisseurs of music, put me entirely in the wrong. I was seated between them, and they would talk across me between the numbers, a habit to which I find the sterner sex far too much addicted.

"I should say," said Mr. Tom, "that this concert is the very worst that has been held these seven years, or for ought I know since the foundation of the society. The players appear to think of nothing but Maelzel's metronome, and do not notice the conductor's *accelerando* or *ritardando*."

"But what can you expect?" asked Mr. Vavasour, "if Cipriani Potter is in command, or Moscheles? The Philharmonic needs a conductor, not a pianist. I yield to no one in admiration for the skill of these gentlemen at their own instrument, but they can hardly excel in conducting as they excel in playing. You may have observed, Miss Dacre, how Mr. Loder, the leader of the orchestra, is not at one with Mr. Watts his next in command, and how Watts refuses to follow Loder's lead. I am extremely sorry for Moscheles. He understands the work of Beethoven which we have just heard, and desires to give the music its full effect, by varying the tempo. But the gentlemen of the orchestra seem to say, 'Pray don't trouble yourself; we are not going to break the time for you or Beethoven, or any one else. What do we care about the music? Are we not paid to play the notes and keep the time?'"

We were now compelled to be silent while Mr. W. Sterndale Bennett played the pianoforte part in a concerto of his own composition for that instrument. Emily was loud in her applause, for two seasons ago she had had lessons from the maestro, but as she tells me that she cried all the time from nervousness, they were of little benefit. A duet by Cinti Damoreau and Mademoiselle Placci from Rossini's *Semiramide,* and an overture by Herr von Weber completed the first part.

During the *entr'acte* Emily mentioned the concerts of Antient Music and expressed a desire to attend one, but Mr. Vavasour firmly dissuaded her.

"The great disadvantage of these concerts," he said, "is that the programmes are drawn up by the directors in rotation, who are all persons of eminence, such as royal dukes, generals, and archbishops, but are not necessarily gifted with a taste for music. They have taken lately to performing airs by Bach, which are rather mechanical dialogues for the voice with some instrument than such airs of expression as made Handel immortal."

"There I cannot agree with you, Vavasour," said Mr. Tom. "There is a degree of sublimity in Bach rarely attained by Handel, whose choruses and arias are apt to degenerate into an almost meaningless jumble of noisy notes."

Mr. Vavasour, not deigning to reply, then asked me how I liked the concert.

"I must confess," said I, "that for my part I find the orchestra a little dull and fatiguing, and would far rather see an opera, where the eye as well as the ear is entertained."

"Then we will go to the Italian Opera at Her Majesty's before you leave town," said Mr. Tom Ingoldsby. "We will make up a party and see Mozart's enchanting *Nozze.* Even you, Vavasour, cannot deny its sweetness and power."

The music then beginning again, we heard a Sinfonia by Mendelssohn Bartholdy, an air from Mozart's *Flauto Magico* sung by Signor Ivanoff, and several other pieces of merit, during which I had great difficulty in resisting a kind of drowsiness. Emily professed to have enjoyed every note: I say *professed.*

I may say that though Emily and I had come to town fully determined to hear as much music as possible, for we are both violently attached to it; we nearly always found something else occupying our time. We did, however, attend Mr. Benedict's concert at the Opera House, and were richly rewarded. It began at half past seven and seemed never to end. Especially wearisome did I find a triple concerto by that Bach, in which Messrs. Benedict, Moscheles, and Doehler played three pianofortes simultaneously. Mr. Tom said that old Sebastian, as he calls him, would have turned in his grave to find himself thus rearranged and instrumented by Moscheles; but how can he tell? I did enjoy Rubini and Lablache in excerpts from Mr. Benedict's opera *The Gipsy's Warning*. M. Lablache teaches our beloved Queen, and this alone is sufficient to place him in the first flight.

The day for Ned's rowing match had now arrived. Emily and I had previously been down to the river, accompanied by Mr. Tom Ingoldsby and Mr. Seaforth, to see the crews practising in their cutters. Ned and his crew wore white jerseys with short sleeves, while Mr. Darnley and his crew had jerseys trimmed with scarlet, and no sleeves, so that Emily and I were really glad that he did not know we were looking at him. I heard the gentlemen laying bets of three to one against Leander, and Mr. Tom asked Emily if she would like to lay a pair of gloves again, but she laughingly declined.

Ned came in to see us the evening before the race, and was as usual unable to talk of anything but his own concerns. I listened as long as I could to his talk of boats and oars, but at last I was fairly driven from the room. When I returned, Ned had gone, and Emily was sitting pensively by the window.

"Tell me, my love," said I, "what had Ned to say?"

"He says they are using the Jesus eight," said Emily, "and that Searle has built a new cutter for the Leander."

"I think," said I, "that it is the letter N that has been too much for you, dear Emily."

At any other time Emily would have shown some spirit at being thus rallied, but she merely replied in an abstracted manner:

"Leander are having oars shorter and lighter than those

generally used, and they have chartered a fast steamer named the *Primrose* for their friends to follow the race, but I am sure that Cambridge will win."

So judging that there was nothing to be made of her, I occupied myself in writing to my dear mother, till it was time to go to bed. Emily was still very absent, and I observed a blue favour in her corsage that certainly had not been there before Ned's visit.

On the following day Mrs. Vavasour called for Emily and me about four o'clock and drove us to the river. As it was impossible for a cutter with a party to keep up with the race, she had ordered her boat to be in readiness a little above Vauxhall Bridge, where we were to pick the crews up and row a short distance with them. We found a small party on board, none of whom except Mr. Vavasour were known to us. Mrs. Vavasour presented one or two gentlemen to Emily, but she was not in her usual spirits and preferred to sit gazing over the rail. The scene was a remarkable one, as the bridge and the banks were black with spectators, and the excitement was universal.

"It is curious to reflect," said Mr. Vavasour, "that of all the poor fellows who are come to witness the match, perhaps not twenty have any connexion with Cambridge, or any interest in the Leander. I confess I am surprised at the multitude of spectators, even if they have money on the match."

A sound of cheering was now wafted to us, and the rival crews came into view. Mr. Vavasour had glasses, and described the progress of the race to me.

"I take it, Miss Harcourt," he said, "that your sympathies are entirely with the boat in which your brother rows."

"Yes, indeed—that is, I suppose so," said I.

"Do not let me bias you against the Cambridge crew," said Mr. Vavasour. "They belong after all to a sister University whose shortcomings one may pity, but should not despise."

"Oh no, indeed," I replied, but he had misunderstood my hesitation. Ned was my brother and as such his success must be dear to me, but there was ONE in the Leander crew, his manly form set off by a white and scarlet jersey, whose fate was not of entire indifference to me.

"Leander do not leave Cambridge room to pass between them and the barges," cried Mr. Vavasour gazing through his glass, "and the Cambridge coxswain has driven his boat full on to Leander's starboard quarter. Now the Cantabs have backed water and their stern has hit the Leander at Number 7. I wager the blow nearly carried his chock away. Now they are passing the Penitentiary, now Leander are away, now Cambridge overhaul them, Leander give them no room to pass—Good God! another foul!"

Here our watermen bent to their oars and Mr. Vavasour resumed his seat with a discomposing suddenness.

"Who is fouling?" I inquired, "Mr. Darnley would never be guilty of so base an action."

"Nor would Mr. Ned Harcourt," sighed Emily.

"I can only conclude," said Mr. Vavasour, his lip curling scornfully, "that the match is being rowed under watermen's rules, which are somewhat like Cornish wrestling—every man for his own hand."

Steadying himself against the side of the boat he resumed his watch.

"Leander are in trouble," he observed. "Number 4's oar has broken, and by heaven! his stopper must have gone. Now a friend from a cutter that accompanies the crews has thrown him another oar."

"See," cried Emily, "Mr. Harcourt's crew are all lifting their oars in the air. What does it mean?"

"I presume they are claiming the race," said Mr. Vavasour, "and indeed Leander's conduct has been of such a description that I consider Cambridge justified in stopping the race."

For a short distance our watermen kept within sight of the crews, but the pace of the rival boats, the immense concourse on the river, and the wash caused by the *Primrose* as she gallantly steamed up Father Thames, caused us to fall behind before we got to the Red House in Battersea Fields.

"Cambridge are trying to drive Leander athwart the bridge, but Parish is manœuvering Leander in fine style," said Mr. Vavasour. "By God, if Leander back water now, Cambridge will go broadside on to the piers and be broken up. No; they get away! Bravo, the Cantabs!"

At this instance of noble impartiality my heart warmed to Mr. Vavasour, and I bestowed a grateful glance on him. A slight shriek caused me to look round, and I saw Emily in an almost unconscious condition.

"Heavens!" I cried, "what is the matter? Mrs. Vavasour, pray come here."

Mrs. Vavasour gave orders to the watermen to return as quickly as possible to the place where the carriage was waiting, and while I supported Emily, our hostess held salts to her nose, and she began to revive.

"Where is Mr. Harcourt?" she cried faintly.

"Why, my dear, Fanny's father did not accompany us today," said Mrs. Vavasour. "You are still confused."

A blush of deepest hue overspread Emily's face and bosom, and she was unable to say a word. I alone understood the cause of her emotion, and under the pretence of adjusting her bonnet I whispered,

"The Cambridge boat got safely through the bridge, and has by now doubtless won the race."

Emily gave me a grateful look and pressed my hand. We had now arrived at the steps, and as Mr. Vavasour handed us to the carriage he observed to me,

"When Beauty and Compassion go hand in hand, Admiration can but be silent."

This was gratifying, showing me as it did that my sisterly attentions to Emily had not passed unnoticed. But I daresay if Mr. Darnley had been there he would have been equally struck, though he does not express himself in so lofty a style as Mr.

Vavasour. Mrs. Vavasour drove us to our lodgings, and her nephew asked permission to call upon us next morning and inquire after Emily's health, and assure himself that my exertions on her behalf had not fatigued me.

I persuaded Emily to go early to bed, and read aloud to her from Bulwer's *Ernest Maltravers*. When I came to the description of the hero's father, I paused.

"'Handsome Hal Maltravers, the darling of the clubs,'" I repeated aloud. "Emily, of whom does that remind you?"

"Your brother is indeed handsome," said she, "and very like you. But he is hardly a clubman yet."

"Ned?" I exclaimed, "you are joking, Emily. Ned is a dear fellow, but no beauty."

"Then, it is Mr. Darnley you mean! He is Hal," said Emily.

"But not to me," I faltered.

"Fanny, I declare you are blushing," said Emily. "Does the thought of Mr. Darnley cause you such emotion?"

It was dusk, the candles were not lighted, and the hour was favourable for confidence. Emily and I spoke freely. I confessed to her that though Mr. Vavasour exercised a deep attraction on me, yet with Mr. Darnley I felt an ease that compensated for his less romantic appearance.

"I could elope with Vavasour," said I, "but I could live with Darnley!"

"And I could do both with your brother," said Emily, covering her face with her hands. But these confidences are sacred.

Next day our two aquatic heroes came to see us. Ned looked sadly done up, and I offered them some wine and refreshments.

"Oh, good God, Fanny, not wine," said Ned with a groan. "Soda-water by the gallon, if you love me."

I rang the bell. Matthews, bringing the soda-water, also announced Mr. Vavasour.

"Good morning ladies," said he, and then addressing himself to Ned and Mr. Darnley, added, "Well, I hear all bets are off."

MY SOUVENIR OF THE CORONATION FAIR

THE QUEEN'S RETURN FROM WESTMINSTER ABBEY, June 28th 1838

RETURN FROM THE CORONATION

"What do you mean?" asked Emily. "Did not Mr. Harcourt—did not Cambridge win?"

"Surely Leander won," said I, looking to Mr. Darnley.

There was a silence. Mr. Darnley and Ned looked at one another and then burst out laughing.

"We may as well confess," said Mr. Darnley. "Our boat was a length ahead at Putney bridge, but somehow Searle, the umpire, did not consider this enough, and after a long argument gave it as no race."

"No more it was," said Ned, who was drinking soda-water to an alarming extent, "because when you Leanders challenged us, we accepted on condition that the race should be rowed under the same rules as it was last year, when we whopped you, that is with no fouling. Oh, Lord, how my throat sizzles!"

"It was your waterman who made the first foul," said Mr. Darnley.

"Searle said Noulton's first foul was accidental," cried Ned. "You heard him yourself. And you heard the fellows shouting in favour of Searle when he gave it no match."

"And you heard the fellows shouting against it," said Mr. Darnley heatedly, "and you cannot deny that Noulton tried to break our rudder, nor that your number 2 laid hold of our boat to try to impede it."

"These are indeed weighty trifles," said Mr. Vavasour, "and quite in the Homeric vein."

Both the gentlemen cast looks of dislike at him, and I confess I thought the remark ill-timed.

"You both look quite done up, to use Ned's expression," said I, addressing the rowers.

"Oh, good Lord, you'd be done up if you'd a head like mine," groaned Ned. "I'll never go to a boating supper again, I swear."

"Were you then celebrating the race with your friends last night to console them for their defeat?" asked Emily tenderly.

"Friends? Oh, Lord, yes, dozens of 'em," said Ned. "Both the crews and all their friends. We were at the Bells Tavern at

Putney, weren't we, Hal? I can't remember anything after Stanley, our stroke, gave 'Health and Prosperity to the Leander Gentlemen.' What happened to me then?"

"You were laid out on three chairs," said Mr. Darnley gravely, "and when the cheering was over, which I thought it never would be, I drove you home in my cab."

"Deuced friendly of you," said Ned, applying himself afresh to the soda-water. "And what a head you have!" he added admiringly.

Mr. Darnley indeed looked just as usual, and I contrasted him favourably in my mind with my father and Ned, who do become so heated with their wine.

"I too have in my time looked upon the wine when it is red, after the boat races at Oxford," said Mr. Vavasour condescendingly, "but I now find that inebriety has few charms, and I daresay the ladies agree."

"I daresay, Vavasour, you feel like a young Spartan among Helots," said Mr. Darnley coolly.

"For my part," cried Emily, "I like a man to show a little spirit."

"Good girl," said Ned, with a familiarity that only his reduced condition could condone. "Hal was as drunk as a lord, only he's such a cool devil he don't show it. Oh, Lord! I'll never do it again!"

"I think," said I, ringing the bell, "Ned had better retire. Matthews, take Mr. Edward upstairs and see him into his bed. Mr. Darnley, you had no business to let Ned behave so foolishly. You are older than he, and it was very unkind, and I thought you had more regard for me. At least you might help Matthews with Ned."

"Allow me, Miss Harcourt," said Mr. Vavasour. "I may not be as athletic as Darnley, but I can assure you of my steadiness."

He sprang forward, but Ned, almost unconscious with the efforts of the previous day and night, said loudly,

"Oh, Lord! Vavasour! I'd as soon have Cockle's Antibilious Pills!" and clinging to Matthews, he stumbled upstairs.

Mr. Darnley then bowed to us and took his leave. He looked pale, and I feared I had hurt him by my hasty words. Willingly would I have called him back, but pride forbade, and it was with an aching heart that I heard his cabriolet drive away.

Mr. Vavasour attempted to raise our spirits, but I am afraid he found us but poor company. He observed that Miss Landon had more merit as a poetess than as a novelist, and spoke slightingly of her book *Ethel Churchill, or The Two Brides*, although it is dedicated to Lady Emmeline Stuart Wortley. He said there were too many historical characters at once in it, such as Pope, Lavinia Fenton, and Lady Mary Wortley Montagu, and that the authoress made too free a use of poison to get her characters off the stage. We both answered so at random that he presently withdrew. When my father came in he inquired after Ned and hearing that he was in bed, sleeping off his excesses, roared with laughter, saying that he was just such a one at his age.

I become rather confused as to all we did for the next ten days. We were engaged almost every hour and every day for some party of pleasure or instruction with the Vavasours, the Ingolds-bys, or other of our acquaintance, and my letters to my dear mother are very short and generally contain the promise, not alas! always fulfilled, to write more in my next. Emily and I were low. Emily had had a private conversation with Ned before he went back to Cambridge. I daresay I should not have allowed it, but then I would not have been able to overhear what they said, the door being just ajar and I being occupied in putting my father's linen in order in the next room. Emily had scolded Ned for having drunk so much at his boating supper, and Ned had accused Emily of preferring Mr. Darnley. On this Emily had burst into tears, and Ned had gone down on his knees, and kissed her hand, calling himself a blackguard and her an angel. At this point I really thought things had gone far enough, so I tiptoed upstairs and then came down humming a careless tune, only to find Ned and Emily at opposite ends of the sitting-room. Ned gave me a little of his confidence as he said good-bye, telling me that Emily was the dearest girl in the world and he was quite unworthy of her. He also, which did not please me so much, begged me not to encourage Mr. Vavasour.

"He's not on the straight, Fan," he said. "He may be a dandy and very literary and all that, but Hal is worth twenty of him."

"Your friend Mr. Darnley is doubtless an estimable young man," said I coldly, "but as I have seen nothing of him for two days, he is to me as if he had never existed."

To this Ned replied, "Gammon," adding that Mr. Darnley had been obliged to return to his country seat on business, and had charged him with messages of apology to me for not having taken a formal leave.

"But cheer up, Fan," said Ned, "Hal will be back before the Coronation, and then we will have famous fun. I shall be down then for good, and ready for anything."

I think it was this week that Upton very inconsiderately had the toothache, and split a bottle of Bond's Marking Ink over one of my father's new shirts, which had to be given to Matthews. Upton went to a dentist in Newman Street and had to have one tooth extracted and one filled with mineral succedaneum, and was quite useless for two days, indeed worse than useless, for she had quarrelled with Mrs. Bellows, and Emily, who is used to visiting the poor, had to look after her, my nerves being too much affected. We also went to see the meeting of the Four-in-Hand Club in Hyde Park, where Emily and I were thrilled to see the famous Count D'Orsay again. My father was in ecstasies over the fine horses, and laid several wagers with other gentlemen on their speed.

"It may interest you, sir," said Mr. Tom Ingoldsby who was with us, "to see the celebrated Count D'Orsay on that second coach."

"Eh?" said my father. "Damned Jacobinical rascal. Thought he had been shot or guillotined years ago."

"I do not quite take your meaning, sir," said Mr. Tom. "Count D'Orsay is quite a young man, barely thirty-five, and could not have been involved in the Revolution."

"Oh, Count D'Orsay," said my father, "why couldn't you say so then? Thought you said Condorcet. *He* was a damned smuggling Frenchman if you like. I daresay this one is too. All foreigners are alike."

Mr. Tom and Ned spent far too much time at the Marylebone Cricket Club, a game which has few attractions for me. They really became so wearisome with their talk about a match against Hampshire that Emily and I were glad to avail ourselves of Mrs. Vavasour's invitation to drive with her to Hampton Court and Kew Gardens, where the pleasure of sauntering under leafy trees and on velvet lawns with Mr. Vavasour was only slightly damped by the presence of Lady Almeria Norbourne, for her ladyship, under pretence of fatigue, but really, as Emily discovered, because her shoes were too tight, preferred to remain in the carriage. All shams are abhorrent to me, and if I have a small foot and a small waist it is no merit of mine, and I would not dream of trying to improve on nature. As Madame Jupon said, by judiciously sewing whalebone into the corsage of my new dress she had reduced my waist to eighteen inches, which was not only becoming, but an inch less than Emily.

CHAPTER 8

WESTMINSTER HALL AND THE OPERA

My father was anxious to show me Westminster Hall. Mr. Vavasour, who is reading for the Bar and is therefore familiar with legal matters, volunteered to be our cicerone, and we had an instructive and exhausting tour.

"I must beg you," said I to Mr. Vavasour, who had come to fetch us, "not to notice Papa. You know his weakness for the past, and how he is quite put out at any changes. I fear that the sight of the proposed new Houses of Parliament may make him fly into one of his rages."

"Do not fear on my account, Miss Harcourt," said Mr. Vavasour.

"Indeed I do not," said I, "it is entirely on my own account and Emily's that I am anxious. You can afford to put up with Papa's ways; you do not have to live with him."

"I cannot think," said Mr. Vavasour, "that Miss Harcourt will remain so long an inmate of her father's house as to have to feel any anxiety for her future peace of mind."

"Lassy me!" cried Emily, "whatever do you mean?"

Mr. Vavasour smiled but made no reply, while Emily gave me a significant look which provoked me very much. My father was then heard roaring for us below stairs, so we went down and took a hackney coach to the bottom of Parliament Street. Here we alighted, and at a hint from Emily Mr. Vavasour paid the coachman, so that my father should not cause the usual morti-fying scene over the fare.

It was one of June's most torrid days, and as we walked towards the New Palace Yard the sun beat upon us with more than tropical ferocity. In front of us lay the object of our visit, to our right was an enclosure planted with trees, beyond which could be seen the tasteful church of St. Margaret's, while the Abbey soared in Gothic splendour above all. Mr. Vavasour insisted that we should step aside a little from our route to observe the fine Gothic building of the New Westminster Hospital, and this was where Emily was splashed by the water-ing cart. This was in itself annoying, for we were not sure whether her silk would spot or not, but Emily need not have talked of nothing else all morning as she did. The man was odiously rude, making remarks about "snobs," and Mr. Vavasour hurried us away. I could not help secretly contrasting his behav-iour with that of Mr. Darnley at the Surrey Zoological Gardens. *He* would have laid the impertinent fellow senseless on the road.

"Let me direct your attention, sir," said Mr. Vavasour, as we approached Westminster's massive pile, "to the improvements that have taken place within the last twenty years. The unsightly inns and coffee houses which used to cluster round the entrance to Westminster Hall have been swept away, and the Law Courts, designed by Sir John Soane, architect of the Bank of England, now balance admirably with the more Gothic taste of Rufus's noble building."

"Improvements, sir!" shouted my father. "What d'ye mean? Many's the frolic I've had in one of those coffee houses you choose to sneer at, when you were eating pap in the nursery, yes, pap, sir. And as for lawyers and Law Courts, what's the country coming to? When I was a young man in London the Lord Chancellor sat in Westminister Hall, and many's the time I've seen him there in his wig. There was no talk of Law Courts then, I can tell you. What was good enough for Lord Eldon isn't good

enough for this Brougham, I dare say, damned Frenchified
Radical I call him."

"You can hardly blame Brougham for the new Law Courts,
sir," said Mr. Vavasour laughing, "for he is hardly Chancellor
except in name, the Great Seal being now in commission. He
occupies himself with writing, and with schemes for the ad-
vancement of popular education."

This was of course another of my dear father's favourite
bugbears, and he inveighed so loudly against education, the
London University, the Society for the Diffusion of Useful
Knowledge, and the new Law Courts, that I was glad when we
passed under the portals of Westminster Hall, where even my
father was silenced. Truly the sight of that great hall, its roof
supported on

Cobwebless beams conceived of Irish oak

which had seen so many stirring scenes of English history,
could not but make one pensive. Emily and I stood in silent
ecstasy, hoping to conceal our ignorance, while Mr. Vavasour
imparted a great amount of useful information to us. I did not
thoroughly grasp all he said, for Emily was still anxious about
the spots on her dress, and I was endeavouring to persuade
her that they were already less unsightly and would shortly
disappear altogether, but it was highly instructive. It is so pleasant to have things told to one, for one need not listen, and yet
feels the benefit of the information. I shall now never forget that
George IV's coronation took place here, whereas our Queen,
with truly religious sentiment, is to be crowned in a sacred fane.
But then there would have been far more impropriety, as Emily
so justly remarked, if Queen Caroline had tried to get into the
Abbey than into a secular building.

I need hardly say that my father was thoroughly put out by
finding that the stalls and bookshops of which he had often told
me were almost a thing of the past. Emily said she could not

understand how lawyers and judges and booksellers could all carry on their business in the same place, and my father took this so much amiss that I began to consider fainting. Turning to see if Mr. Vavasour was at hand, I almost collided with a little sharp-featured shabbily-dressed woman carrying a large reticule. She stopped and looked at me with so piercing a glance that I felt quite confused and asked her pardon.

"Granted, my dear young lady, granted," said she. "I see you are a stranger here and mean no harm. I thought at first you were trying to obstruct my passage. They are always trying to deprive me of my rights, you know. In fact I am on my way to lay a complaint, but the Great Seal is in Commission, so I hardly know where to go at present."

Smiling and waving her hand she passed rapidly on, and disappeared in the direction of the Law Courts.

"Who is that lady?" said I to Mr. Vavasour.

"A very well-known figure here," was his answer. "Her name is Miss R., and she has a delusion about her imaginary rights. She always carries that bag, as big as a coalsack, and has been more than once kind enough to show me the contents, which are of a very miscellaneous nature, including papers, mouldy crusts, bottles of discoloured water, and scraps of rubbish of all kinds. No one knows where or how she lives, but as she is remarkably shrewd except on this one point, she must be able to look after herself."

"Poor creature," said Emily, "does no one ever listen to her?"

"No less a person than the Lord Chancellor himself has listened to her more than once," said Mr. Vavasour. "A few years ago I happened to be strolling about the Courts and came into the Court of Chancery, just as the Chancellor was about to deliver judgement in an important case. A hubbub at the door attracted my attention. It was Miss R., who having eluded the officials at the door, came in crying, 'Justice, justice, in the name of the King of England.' The Chancellor, seized with a sudden fit of benevolence very uncommon in him, leant over his desk, and using the blandest accents asked her, amid the titters of the court, to bring her papers to his private room.

"'I knew I should get justice at last, I knew it,' she said triumphantly, 'or I wouldn't have done for you as much as I did last night.'

"'And what was that?' asked the Chancellor, humouring her.

"'I was obliged to keep Scorpio's tail in Aquarius's bucket all night,' said she confidentially, 'or he would have set fire to your wig.'

"Even the Chancellor's gravity could not resist this, and he laughed heartily. Miss R. no whit disconcerted, curtsied to him and left the court, apparently satisfied."

"Poor thing," said my father, who had been listening to the end of this story. "I'd like to give her a guinea."

Mr. Vavasour offered to convey it to her as delicately as possible, an act which raised him in my favour, though I daresay Mr. Darnley would have done just the same, and added something from his own pocket.

We now left the Hall and walked towards the river, passing on our way the ruins of the old Houses and the beginnings of the new. It appeared that the first step was to construct a river wall, a very costly business. Mr. Vavasour told us that it had been found necessary to dredge out the river and make a coffer dam, so that the foundations of the new embankment might be safely laid on concrete.

"There," said Mr. Vavasour, pointing to various pieces of machinery, barges, and piles which were in picturesque confusion on the banks and in the river, "there you may see the celebrated coffer dam which caused the no less celebrated eddy, source of much of the very childish wrangling in the match between Cambridge and Leander. As the dam has now been almost a year in the making, it is idle to deny that every waterman on these reaches knows every current at high and low tide, so the talk of a foul was mere folly."

Emily and I were coldly silent. Neither Mr. Darnley nor Ned

would have mentioned the coffer dam unless it were of some real importance in the race, and Mr. Vavasour had no right to speak so slightingly of clubs to which he does not belong. Not that I know in the least what a coffer dam is, but if Mr. Darnley does, surely that is enough.

"Well, I dare say," said my father, "they'll have run up these new buildings by next year and then perhaps the Tories will come in again. The Radicals burnt the old Houses, so Melbourne must find the money to build the new ones, and then Peel can take possession of 'em."

"I fail to follow your argument, sir," said Mr. Vavasour, with that hauteur of which Oxonians possess the secret to a high degree, "but I fear it will be many years before Mr. Barry can finish the rebuilding. Possibly Sir Robert may be dead before he can enter into his inheritance."

My father stared and muttered something about young puppies, but did not pursue the subject.

"I may tell you," added Mr. Vavasour to my father, "that all the attacks that have been made upon Barry, the architect of these proposed buildings, have come through Mr. Hume, so doubtless you will agree that Barry is the best choice that could have been made."

"I really think those spots have entirely gone," cried Emily, looking at her dress in the sunlight.

"I told you they would, my love," said I. "When we get back Upton shall press the breadth with a warm iron, and you will never know that the accident occurred."

Having thus exhausted the interest of Westminster, we took coach to our lodgings again, and parted from Mr. Vavasour, with many thanks, until the day of the Coronation, when we were to meet him at the Athenaeum Club in Pall Mall.

On talking over the events of the day, Emily and I agreed that Miss R. would make an admirable subject for our dear Boz. It is a tribute to his genius that whenever I meet a peculiar character his name rises unbidden to my mind. How I wish that he could see Miss R. and give her a page in one of his immortal works. Emily said that the Court of Chancery would also form an admirable subject for his glowing pen, but I pointed out to her that his genius for describing courts of law lies more in the comic, as in the inimitable scenes in Pickwick, and Emily saw the force of my argument. I am glad to say that the stains disappeared from Emily's dress as if they had never been there, and after Upton had ironed it, it looked as good as new.

As the Coronation day drew nigh, a general state of excitement prevailed. Workmen were beginning to put up barriers to prevent the traffic from entering Piccadilly and the other streets on the route, and every shop was selling Coronation bonnets, or tablecloths, or biscuits. Hearing that the Crown and the other jewels were on show at Messrs. Rundell and Bridges, we made up a party to go, but by the time we arrived at Ludgate Hill there was such a block that we decided to go the last few hundred yards on foot, and even so it was only with difficulty that we made our way into the shop, and I was too cross to enjoy the spectacle of glittering splendour. The state of the traffic is quite dreadful, and within a few years it will be impossible to move at all.

On the evening of this day my father invited the Ingoldsbys and Seaforths, and Mrs. and Mr. Vavasour to visit us. A note had also been sent to Mr. Darnley's club, but no answer had been received. However, my spirits were raised by Ned's arrival, with a quantity of luggage and a fine pointer, who leapt upon us in a truly endearing way. We were afraid that Mrs. Bellows might object to her, but luckily she is one of those landladies in whose eyes young men can do no wrong, and at a word from Ned she expressed her entire willingness to allow the dog to sleep in Ned's room and be fed in the kitchen.

"And what is his name, sir?" she inquired.

"She's a bitch," said Ned with a loud laugh, "and her name's Emily."

"Really, sir," said Mrs. Bellows, "well now, if that isn't quite a squinstance, her having the same name as Miss Dacre, though it don't seem natural for a dog to be a she."

"That's all right, Mother B., don't you poke your handsome nose into what isn't your business," said Ned, at the same time clasping her round the ample waist and giving her a hearty kiss, at which she told him to give over, and with apologies to us went downstairs in high good humour.

"I say, Emily," said Ned, "I hope you don't think it infernal presumption to call the bitch Emily. She's the dearest thing you ever knew, sits on my knees like a child and spends the night on my bed. Oh, I say, confound it, Emily, don't be offended."

For Emily, divided between confusion and amusement, had risen and was preparing to leave the room.

"Damn it all," continued poor Ned, "I meant no harm, and I know I'm not much good at speeches, but Em, you do forgive me, don't you? I'll blow my brains out if you don't."

"Don't do that, Ned," said I, "or Emily will pine away. She nearly fainted when she thought your boat was going to be overturned."

At this Ned hit himself and called himself a brute, and I considered it better to leave them alone, so I put on my hat and shawl and went round to Mivart's, where I spent an hour with Mrs. Seaforth, who told me all about her elder children, Neddy, Mary Anne, and Julia. I hinted to her that there might be something between Emily and Ned, and she became quite animated.

"I am quite pleased," said she in her gentle way, "because I thought Hal Darnley might be attached to Emily, but he would be quite unsuitable for her. She has been used to having her own way, and she and Mr. Darnley would not hit it off at all. Now I know exactly who would suit him, but wild horses would not drag it from me."

Though I am not a wild horse I teased her to tell me what she meant, but all in vain.

"I will only tell you," said she, "that the sixth letter of the alphabet is Darnley's favourite."

With this I was forced to be content, and went back to Queen Street to find Emily pensive but serene.

After dinner the Vavasours arrived, shortly afterwards followed by the Ingoldsby party, among whom, to my great relief, was Mr. Darnley. Old Mr. Ingoldsby was in a state of great indignation.

"Why, whatever is the matter, sir?" asked Emily, who as I have before mentioned is a great favourite with the old gentleman.

"Matter, my dear?" said he, "Matter enough. Brooks's Club, my club you know, wished to show their loyalty by having a grand ball in honour of the Coronation. To make it more of an occasion our Committee was empowered to ask Boodle's and White's to join with us. And what d'ye think they answered?"

"A ball, father? How charming!" said Mrs. Seaforth. "I shall not of course dance," said she, looking tenderly upon Mr. Seaforth, who appeared to wish that she would not, "but I shall certainly be present."

"You'll find it difficult, my girl, to be present at something that doesn't exist," said her father. "Boodle's and White's declined the invitation, confound 'em for supercilious Tories!"

"Quite right too," cried my father, slapping his leg in his annoying way, and how I wish I could persuade him to give up his breeches and boots and take to trousers as every one else has done these I don't know how many years is only known to my Creator and myself. "Why should loyal clubs wait for the Whigs to give 'em a lead? If White's wants a ball, it will have one. Confounded impertinence, I call it."

"I may mention," said Mr. Darnley, "that the Reform was not even honoured by an invitation."

"I should think not," said Mr. Ingoldsby. "If you Radicals can stomach a man like Fox, you need showing your place. Did you see Publicola's last article on the Royal Touch, Harcourt?"

Luckily my father had seen it. I say luckily, because it proved a bond of reunion between him and Mr. Ingoldsby, and in vilifying Publicola and the Radicals they forgot to feel indignant or exultant over the projected ball.

"We do not give balls at the Athenaeum," said Mr. Vavasour to Emily, loftily, but Mr. Ingoldsby unfortunately heard the remark and said, loud enough to be heard, that a ball given by a set of literary puppies would indeed be a comical affair.

"This is indeed a shocking business about the explosion on the steamship *Victoria*, Mr. Ingoldsby," said I, anxious to avert another explosion! "They say the poor fellows who were near the boiler were mutilated in a manner impossible to describe."

At this my father went off in one of his transports about steam, vowing that a few more explosions would convince people that they ought to stick to sails and roads instead of boilers and rails. He added that he hoped the same fate would attend Mr. Hancock's steam cab which we had recently seen in Hyde Park, and dwelt with some pleasure upon the appalling accidents which had lately taken place upon the American steamboats. It is useless to contradict my father when he is well launched upon his favourite subject, but Mrs. Vavasour, who seems to have a special *penchant* for him, suggested a game of cards, to which after some grumbling he consented to sit down with her, Mr. Ingoldsby, and Mr. Seaforth.

Mr. Vavasour now remarked that he had been much shocked by an article in the *Quarterly Magazine* which he understood to be by Mr. Croker, a Tory writer, in which, on pretence of reviewing a book about the Peninsular War, he took occasion to traduce Marshal Soult, who was to be Ambassador from France at the coming festivities.

"I understand," said he, "that the Duke did his best to get Croker to delay publishing this article till the next number, for fear that Soult might feel the intended insult, but Croker would not hear of it. I do not pretend to judge, I am merely a poor novelist, more concerned with the emotions of hearts and the trifles that make up our society than with wars or generals, but there is such a thing as Good Taste. An ancient enemy is to visit us in the garb of peace, accredited representative of a friendly government. All rancour should be laid aside, and to write as Croker has written is really not quite what a man would choose to do. *Noblesse oblige.*"

I feared that my father would interpose with his usual statement that one Englishman can beat three Frenchmen, but the cards held his attention. We all agreed that Mr. Croker's conduct was indeed shocking, irrespective of party feeling.

"At least, by arriving on the 19th, Marshall Soult misses the Waterloo celebrations," said Mr. Vavasour. "For one of Napoleon's marshals to witness the rejoicings on the anniversary of his former master's defeat would indeed be mortifying."

"It isn't all beer and skittles though, Vavasour," said Mr. Tom Ingoldsby, who had been cutting out my poor Ned with Emily, and tired of this pastime was looking for someone else to provoke. "Soult may have missed Waterloo on the 18th, but he falls into the anniversary of Vittoria on the 21st, and will have to hurry back to avoid the anniversaries of Talavera, Salamanca, and the Battle of the Nile."

Mr. Tom's droll way of saying this raised a general laugh.

"By the way, Miss Harcourt," said Mr. Tom, "you remember my pointing out to you at Epsom M. de Melcy, the husband of Grisi the singer?"

I signified my recollection of the fact.

"I suppose you have heard of his duel with Lord Castlereagh," said Mr. Tom.

"Oh, pray tell us about it," said Emily, Mrs. Seaforth, and I in chorus.

"Well, it seems," said Mr. Tom, "that his lordship has been sweet on the Grisi for a long time, and he used to hang about the house and send her notes. One of these fell into M. de Melcy's hand so what could he do but challenge the *innamorato?* Castlereagh, to do him justice, seems to have behaved with coolness and spirit. He took up the challenge, and the duel came off at the Wormwood Scrubs. His lordship had a ball through his arm which grazed his chest, and honour was satisfied."

"Well, I say Lord Castlereagh was acting very wrongly," said Mrs. Seaforth, "to send notes to a married woman, even if she were a singer. Charles would challenge any one who sent a note to me, would you not, Charles?"

"No, my dear," said Mr. Seaforth, looking up from his game, "In the first place I am—or was—a soldier, and don't care to risk my life when I needn't. In the second place I have every confidence in your virtue, and in the third place I believe you would be too lazy to read a *billet doux* and would make it into paper boats or cocked hats for the children."

"Bravo, Charles!" cried Mr. Tom. "That is Caroline to a T!"

"For my part," said Mr. Vavasour, "I consider the whole affair a put-up job. De Melcy is an adventurer and out to make what he can."

"At least, Vavasour, you must admit," said Mr. Darnley, who had hitherto been silent, "that the Grisi's conduct is generally considered as unexceptionable, and I have it on the best authority that Lord Castlereagh left a letter, to be opened in case of his death, stating that she never gave him the slightest encouragement."

"Did you see the poem in *Bell's Life?*" asked Ned, from the corner where he was now comfortably ensconced with Emily.

"Pray tell us," said Mrs. Seaforth.

"It's a long affair," said Ned, "and some of it's a bit h'm, h'm. But the end is good. It runs:

> Young lordships scorched by Cupid's flames,
>   Let foreigners alone,
> And don't be sweet on married dames,
>   Unless they are your own.

Famous, isn't it?"

"It is indeed," said Emily, just as if Ned had written it himself. Music was now called for and Emily played the *Telegraphe Musicale,* a Grand Pot-Pourri of Waltzes by Strauss, to which she had given much study of late. Mr. Tom Ingoldsby sang some very amusing comic songs with much spirit, and Mr. Seaforth, who had luckily brought his flute, played some airs from Donizetti's *Parisina,* which made us wish we could see that *chef d'œuvre.* I then, though unwillingly, and not till Mr. Vavasour had repeatedly pressed me, sang Haydn's tuneful canzonetta, "She never told her love." I did not quite know to whom I addressed the palpitating words, but Emily told me afterwards that I had never sung with such expression. We terminated the *soirée musicale* by Bishop's glee, "Sleep, Gentle Lady," during which I distinctly heard Mr. Darnley singing the words, "Weep, Zegri Ladye", accompanied by a glance in my direction which caused my cheeks to burn. My father, having been diverted from his purpose of singing "A frog he would a-wooing go!", our party made their farewells and retired. I wish Mr. Darnley were a member of the Athenaeum club.

Emily and I did several daring deeds while in London, such as going in a sixpenny bus to Battersea, just for the fun of it, and accompanying Mrs. Bellows to Mr. Kipling's Warehouse where Emily bought six dozen pairs of stockings for the parish at a very reasonable rate. We also made up a party with Mr. Tom Ingoldsby and Ned to see the *Parisina* with whose notes Mr. Seaforth's flute had charmed us. We were partly actuated by a wish to see Grisi, the heroine of the late duel, and partly by hearing that the Queen would be present. Emily had been to Her Majesty's Theatre on previous occasions, but the Theatre Royal, Norwich, was my highest dramatic flight, so I was delighted to see a metropolitan opera house. The opera of *Parisina* was musical in the extreme, though we thought Grisi labouring under a sense of her embarrassing position, and our chief applause was reserved for the ballet. Between the acts Teresa and Fanny Elsler appeared amid hurricanes of applause. The way in which Fanny slides across the stage on her toes is unprecedented, and we were enraptured. I must say though that their costumes, though elegant, were light to a degree that was almost objectionable, and we gathered from the shouts and calls in our neighbourhood that the sentiment was general. Luckily I could not make out what the noisier members of the audience were saying, and the word "Cherubim," which seemed to raise a laugh, appeared to me meaningless. After the opera the great dancer Taglioni appeared in a *pas de deux* with Guerra, and this was followed by another ballet, *The Brigand of Terracina,* in which the two Elslers appeared. Mr. Ingoldsby said he had preferred Duvernay in the elegant waltz scene in the robbers' cavern. We did not exactly see the Queen, but we heard the tumultuous applause which greeted her and were gratified to feel ourselves so near.

I shall not easily forget the scene when we got back. My dear father had also, though unknown to us, been at the opera, and had seen us. It was certainly not our fault that the Elslers were insufficiently or inappropriately clad, but my father behaved as if it were, threatening to take me home and pack Emily back to Tapton if we went to a ballet again without his permission. I do not pretend to be a philosopher, but I know my dear father well enough to take his moods as they come, and merely answered, "Yes, Papa," and "No, Papa," to his scoldings, till he grew tired. I mentioned the presence of Her Majesty, but this he averred, with an oath, to be a piece of Whiggish intrigue and told me to hold my tongue. Emily and I decided as we undressed that we would get married as soon as possible, though merely as an abstract idea and naming no names.

It was a night or two after that, my father being out of town for two or three days, that Mr. Tom Ingoldsby carried out his promise of taking Emily and me to Mozart's *Nozze.* This work is one which appeals to the intellectual as well as the sensual organs, and in consequence the press of people anxious to see it was terrifying. Mr. Tom had taken the precaution of buying tickets beforehand from Mitchell's Library in Bond Street, but even so we were almost swept off our feet, in spite of the protection of Mr. Vavasour, Mr. Tom, and Mr. Darnley. The rush to gain admission was quite appalling, partly I fear from a vulgar sentiment of curiosity to see Grisi. Before the performance commenced the house and the space behind the scenes was densely packed with people. Women shrieked, ruffianly men elbowed and shoved, the manager was forced to make an appeal for quiet, announcing that admission money would be refunded to those who could not find accommodation. Never have I beheld such disgusting violence and un-called-for brutality as among those so-called music-lovers.

The opera itself ravished me, though Mr. Tom said it was insufficiently rehearsed. Grisi in the role of Susanna was naïve and vivacious, Persiani as the Countess ladylike and dignified, and their duet, *Sull'aria,* brought tears to my eyes. Mr. Tom remarked that Albertazzi as Cherubino was not unlike Boz's Fat Boy, which made Emily and me give way to unseemly mirth. Tamburini as the Count had taste and spirit, but what can I say of Lablache? His *Non più andrai* electrified me, and in the concerted music he was imbued with the true Promethean fire. Fanny Elsler, *suitably* attired, danced a Cachucha in the opera, and afterwards we were given the last scene from Donizetti's *Lucia,* and were delighted by the elegant evolutions of Taglioni in a Tyrolienne, which closed the proceedings at a very late hour.

We chose to walk home, the night being fine. Mr. Vavasour hummed as we walked, "Crudel, perchè," in a meaning way, and I, carried away by the music we had heard, went so far as to join in a few notes of the duet. I would not have done this if Mr. Darnley had been there, but as he had chosen to go back to his club, I felt at liberty to please myself. Oh, Music! Daughter of Jove!

CHAPTER 9
CORONATION DAY

The day before the Coronation we strolled through the streets with the Ingoldsbys to view the last preparations. The town had a gay and festive air. Stands were erected in front of many of the clubs and shops, and workmen were putting the finishing touches to the illuminations. Even by daylight the hundreds of coloured lamps were a very pretty spectacle, and if the gas jets were not so gay by day, they filled me with the liveliest anticipations for the night. We were told that the Ordnance Office in Pall Mall alone had sixty thousand lamps, so what the total number in town must have been, I cannot conceive. I saw from an advertisement in *The Times* that coloured lamps were to be had for half a crown a dozen, so the expense may be partially guessed. We walked along Piccadilly as far as Hyde Park Corner and saw the stands erected outside St. George's Hospital, from the proceeds of which it is to be hoped that the patients will benefit. I had had half a thought of procuring tickets there and sending Matthews and Upton, but reflecting that they could see just as well from the street, I refrained.

On the following morning, the long-awaited twenty-eighth of June, a Thursday, Emily and I were awoken by the noise of cannon at four o'clock. To our consternation it was raining! Our first thought was for ourselves and our dresses, our second for the poor Queen. However, much may happen in the space of several hours, as Emily remarked, so we dressed ourselves with what philosophy we could, Upton having had permission to go out as early as possible in order to obtain a good place for the procession.

Mr. Vavasour had informed us that there was to be a breakfast at the Athenaeum from 7.30 till 10, so we sallied forth shortly after seven, determined to be in time. Smart showers had been falling at intervals, and we feared for the condition of the streets, but so well had they been strewn with gravel along the line of the route, that we were sensible of very little inconvenience. My father, who proposed to spend the day at White's, accompanied us as far as the Athenaeum, which is a fine building in the classical style, surmounted by a Grecian frieze. As the regular police force would be fully occupied, a number of special constables had been sworn in. These had tapes tied round their wrists to distinguish them from the crowd, and we heard many derisive or abusive shouts of "Tapemen" from the mob, which, though good-humoured, was not disposed to pay very much attention to these temporary officers of the law.

Although it was so early it was already difficult to get along some of the streets, and from remarks that we heard in the crowd we gathered that many people had arrived at five o'clock or even earlier in order to obtain a place in the front rank. Here we witnessed a very ludicrous occurrence. One of the new cabs with a door at the back was proceeding down St. James's Street. The vehicle which followed it was drawn by a large black horse, whose driver could only with difficulty hold him in. As the crush in the road increased, the black horse, pressed from the rear, made a plunge forward and put his head in at the door of the cab. His driver pulled him back, and no damage was done, but what was our amusement to see an elderly gentleman in court dress put his face out at the door and stare gravely into the countenance of the quadruped who had so rudely intruded upon him. The crowd cheered loudly. The elderly gentleman took off his hat, bowed, and retired once more into the cab. These little incidents are all part of that diversified whole which is London.

The clubs in St. James's Street and Pall Mall were indeed a triumph of the decorator's art. Nearly every house had its front hidden by wooden galleries, tastefully draped with material of various hues. Crockford's in particular made a magnificent display, and we observed that the galleries everywhere were mostly filled by members of the fair sex, the gentlemen preferring the windows. Among those buildings which were in remarkable taste I may mention English's Hotel at the corner of Pall Mall, the United University Club, and the Carlton Club, where elegant balconies were raised from the two floors, and filled with company evidently of the highest order.

Outside the Athenaeum Club Mr. Vavasour was waiting, and he conducted us to our places on the stand, which were facing Pall Mall and commanded an excellent view of the route. They were also sheltered by a canopy, affording a grateful protection from both rain and sun. The streets, which had earlier been like a sea of umbrellas, now became visible in all their glory, as the sun struggled forth, to take his share in honouring our young Queen. On the stand we found Mrs. Vavasour, who inquired whether we had breakfasted, and hearing that we had been too much excited to take more than a cup of tea, conducted us to the room where a breakfast was being served. Mr. Vavasour informed us that ladies were the only strangers privileged to be admitted to the club on this occasion, and that over a thousand of the fairer sex, in many cases accompanied by one or more of their offspring, were present, besides about four hundred members of the club.

While we were eating, Mr. Vavasour pointed out several celebrities to us, one of whom was that odious Mr. Croker who wrote so vilely about Marshal Soult. On being told who he was I took a violent dislike to him and luckily had occasion to show it. He reached across me in a very impertinent manner to obtain something from the buffet, upon which, with many apologies, I contrived so to jog his elbow that the contents of his plate were upset, and I had the satisfaction of seeing a jelly fall onto his boots. He looked at me with an expression that would have annihilated any poor author whose book he was to review, but as I was perfectly unknown to him and had no fear of being *cut up* in the *Quarterly*, I could meet his glance with disdain. Mr. Vavasour, who had observed the scene, could not help smiling.

"I see, Miss Harcourt," said he, "that you are a doughty champion of our friendly enemy Marshal Soult. If he knew how valiantly you had avenged him, he would venture to make a special bow in your direction when he passes in the procession. Would," he added in a lower tone, "that Miss Harcourt could be at hand when the *Quarterly* reviews *Jocelyn FitzFulke.*"

"That reminds me, Mr. Vavasour," said I, "that I have never yet had the courage to speak to you about your novel. I cannot tell you how much Miss Dacre and I admire it. But it was very wrong to enclose the verses. Imagine my feelings if any one had seen them."

"We poor poets," said Mr. Vavasour, bending over me so that his curls almost touched my face, "must needs speak the truth, though we flaunt every convention. If my verses offended Miss Harcourt, I can but apologize, deeply and humbly. But I think I see in your eyes that I am forgiven, am I not?"

I turned away in confusion and at that moment Emily approached us.

"Oh, Mr. Vavasour," said she, "you know every one. Pray who is the gentleman with the very auburn hair who looks as if he were some one? See, there he is, talking to a lady in violet silk."

"He is indeed some one," said Mr. Vavasour, "and so is his fair companion. You have picked out perhaps two of the most interesting of the stars in our literary galaxy. The gentleman is Mr. Bulwer, the lady Mrs. Norton."

"Lassy me!" cried Emily, thus disgracing me publicly, but it is of no use speaking to Emily, though there are moments when I could willingly pretend that I did not know her.

"My aunt will, I am sure, have great pleasure in presenting

you to Mrs. Norton," said Mr. Vavasour. "I will find her at once."
Before I could protest he had left us. What was I to do? Mr.
Darnley had intimated that she was not the person a young
unmarried woman should know, and Mr. Darnley's good opinion was dear to me. On the other hand, Mr. Darnley was far
away at the Reform Club, mixing with his Radical friends, and
need never know.

"What shall we do?" said I to Emily.

"Lord!" said Emily, "you are not thinking of what Darnley
said, are you? My dearest Fanny, do not put on the country
mouse. Mrs. Norton's books are read by every one, and what
harm can it do to speak to her? If Darnley were your husband it
would be different, but he has no right to dictate to you whom
you may meet. I must say I would like to see what a female writer
who is separated from her husband is like."

Emily's indelicacy really shocked me, but as her sentiments
coincided with my own, I said nothing. Mr. Vavasour now
returned with his aunt, who led Emily and me to the two
celebrities. Emily, I regret to say, made a *dead set* at Mr. Bulwer,
plying him with the most outspoken flattery, to which, like most
of his sex, he did not seem averse. I was therefore left *tête-à-tête*
with Mrs. Norton.

"Are you happy, Miss Harcourt?" she asked, fixing her large
expressive eyes on me.

This was such a difficult question to answer that I stood dumb
before her. I felt I ought to be unhappy, but could not think of
any sufficient cause.

"I have embarrassed you, child," said she. "You must forgive
me. Perhaps I touch a tender chord."

"Not at all, madam," said I, not quite knowing how to address
an honourable, especially one in her peculiar position, "I am
afraid you will think me very stupid not to be unhappy, but it is
all Mr. Vavasour's fault, who would be kind enough to ask his
aunt to present me. I would never have presumed to address the
author of *The Sorrows of Rosalie*."

"You like my poems then?" asked Mrs. Norton eagerly.

Luckily I had procured and read a copy after Mr. Darnley had spoken so strongly against her, and I must say I had thought the poems were full of feeling.

"Oh, indeed I do," said I. "They are so like what one thinks oneself, only one could never have said it so well. The poem which begins, 'I do not love thee!' struck me particularly."

"Poor child," said Mrs. Norton, gazing at me with compassion, "is that then your feeling? My own heart has long since turned to stone, but I can yet feel for the young and ardent. If it is Vavasour, I pity you indeed. He would be another Norton. He would brush the bloom from the flower and leave it, broken, to face a cold world. Look at me, Miss Harcourt, and take warning."

I did look at her, but she was so beautiful and so exquisitely dressed that it was difficult to divine the canker that was doubtless gnawing at her heart. Her way of speaking of Mr. Vavasour made me rather uncomfortable, and I was glad when she turned to some other friends. I then made my way to Emily, who was all excitement.

"Imagine, my dear Fanny," she cried, "Mr. Bulwer has told me that he is to bring out a sequel to *Ernest Maltravers!* You remember the orphan Alice, whom Ernest adopted or worse, at least I suppose it was worse, for the child appears to have been his, and how she met him at an inn in after years and fainted at his sight, though he did not see her. Well, he is to write a continuation of her story, and it is to be called *Alice, or the Mysteries,* and it is to have all sorts of things in it. What did Mrs. Norton say to you?"

"Do not ask me, Emily," said I impressively, "and whatever you do, do not let Mr. Darnley know that I met her. Remember, I have never let my father suspect that there is any understanding between you and Ned."

Emily laughed and pressed my hand.

It was now high time to take our seats for the procession,

which was to leave the New Palace at ten o'clock. A gun announced that the Queen had started, and as the moments passed and the sound of cheering began to reach our ears, we became violently excited. How can I describe our sensations as we saw the first soldiers turning the corner of St. James's Street, and riding proudly along Pall Mall? It would be idle to attempt to describe the glittering throng, for my children may read the account for themselves in the newspapers of the day, but I must mention a few circumstances which seemed to me peculiarly noteworthy.

Our chief interest, apart from our young sovereign, was Marshal Soult, the Duke of Dalmatia. Let no tongue of calumny say that Britons are not magnanimous to a noble foe. The cheers that rent the welkin as the French Ambassador's coach came in sight were positively deafening, and every rank appeared to vie in doing honour to our whilom enemy. His coach, which Mr. Vavasour told me was one of the old Bourbon equipages, was painted a rich cobalt relieved with gold, and had a lamp with a massive silver coronet at each corner, while the harness and furniture were white and silver. We could only catch a glimpse of the celebrated warrior himself, but we could see that he had a dark complexion and was of a considerable age.

"Long live Soult!" burst from the crowd, some saying Sowlt and some Soolt, "huzza, huzza!" I added my voice to the general tumult, flags were waved from every balcony, and Emily agitated her scarf so violently that I was obliged to look as if she did not belong to my party. By the time the Queen's carriage arrived my eyes were so full of tears of emotion that I could hardly see her, and many must have shared my feelings. I also saw with emotion the Duchess of Kent, whose maternal heart must have been filled with pride on that eventful day.

When the last of the carriages had passed, there was a general movement. Mr. Vavasour suggested that we should take a stroll in the Park while the Royal party were in the Abbey, which we accordingly did. The Ambassadors' carriages were ranged in the

Bird Cage Walk and were magnificent in the extreme. The coachmen and other servants had thrown off their dignity and were sitting or standing about, cocked hats and wigs off, smoking their pipes or partaking of refreshment. We met several of our acquaintance here, including a Quaker lady from Norwich, who presented us to Miss Caroline Fox, a lively lady of the same persuasion. I have ever been friendly towards the Quakers, who abound near my father's seat in Norfolk. They seem to be a useful and philanthropic sort of persons, and as for their religion, I have been brought up an Anglican and can tolerate any form of worship which does not attempt to foment discord among the lower orders. As the Quakers have no lower orders to speak of, being wonderfully blessed with the good things of this world, they can never constitute a menace to society. Miss Fox pointed out to us the Belgian Ambassador's carriage, which though it was very grand, yet had part of the harness tied up with string. We observed that in the park a chair was being hired for five shillings and a table for twenty. Miss Fox told us that it was computed that over two hundred thousand pounds had been spent on seats alone.

Her Majesty was expected to pass down Pall Mall again about 4 o'clock, and long before that time we were settled in our places. Here we had occasion to admire the discipline of the police. The crowd, who had stood all day in considerable heat, and had indulged in deep potations, began to get restive, and we were apprehensive that some might break through the line of march. The police were, however, more than equal to the occasion, and turned the open space near the Athenaeum into a kind of penal settlement, for no sooner did an offender make himself so conspicuous as to become their captive, than he was forthwith consigned to that particular station.

The return of the procession did not greatly differ from what we had already seen, and after the fatigue of the day we were ready enough to go to our lodgings. One incident I must mention which showed that Britons are yet Hearts of Oak. As we were making our way homewards through the crowd under Mr. Vavasour's escort, we heard a noise which appalled me, the noise of an angry mob booing and hissing. I shrank closer to Mr. Vavasour, who drew us into a doorway. Here, standing on the step, he could better see what was going on.

"They are hissing O'Connell," said he to us, "and I must applaud the good old English spirit which makes the crowd hoot such a dangerous demagogue as the so-called Liberator. If I stand for Parliament as I shall probably do, I shall oppose such men in every way in my power."

"But do authors get into Parliament?" asked Emily.

"I might mention among contemporary author-politicians," said Mr. Vavasour, "Disraeli, whom you met the other night, Bulwer, Macaulay, who by the way returns from India this summer, and is sure to be in the House next year, and half a dozen more equally well known. Because we are poor scribblers, Miss Dacre, our hearts are not the less patriotic."

When we reached our door, I ventured to ask Mr. Vavasour if he would join us at the Ingoldsbys' that evening, but he replied with seemingly real regret that he was engaged to go with his aunt and Lady Almeria Norbourne to a musical party.

"But I trust I may see Miss Harcourt again before long," he said. "The acquaintance—or may I presume to say the friendship—of the last few weeks cannot be permitted to languish. I might say more, but this is hardly the time, nor the place. Miss Harcourt, may I see you tomorrow, when I am less agitated?"

While hardly seeing any cause for agitation, I gave the desired permission, and running upstairs, told Emily what had been said.

"Depend on it, Fanny," said she, "Mr. Vavasour is going to propose to you. I am not surprised, but I shall regret it if you accept him."

"Why so?" I asked. "Not that I for a moment anticipate that he will do any such thing."

"My dearest Fanny," replied Emily, "it is difficult to be explicit without embarrassment. I will only observe that whether I marry or not, Tapton must be my home as long as my father lives, and that Tapton Hall is within a few minutes' walk of the Rectory. If my Fanny is to live in London, I shall see her but seldom."

"This is indeed a most improper conversation," said I, "but I must say, with as much delicacy as possible, that if you and Ned do make a match of it, your home will be in Norfolk after your father's death, and Norfolk is farther from London than Kent."

We agreed that it is impossible to foretell what has not yet occurred, but our philosophical confabulation was interrupted by Mrs. Bellows and Upton, who had just returned from Hyde Park Corner, where they had stood for nearly ten hours and obtained an excellent view of the procession.

"I'm sure you'll excuse me and Mrs. Upton coming in like this, miss," said Mrs. Bellows, whose good-natured countenance was almost purple with her exertions, "but I thought you'd like to know we was back."

"I hope you had good places," said I.

"Indeed we did, miss, being as I have my nephew, my own younger sister's son as you might say, working as porter at St. George's Hospital. They had closed the hospital for the day, unless it was for any poor creature that got hurt in the crowd, so my nephew was able to get off duty for a bit and he got us with our backs nicely up against the hospital wall and fetched us a couple of stools, so that we could see over the people's heads. Lor, miss, what do you think happened? It put me all of a tremble. There was a great ugly bird flying backwards and forwards, and I said to Mrs. Upton 'Depend upon it, Mrs. Upton, that's a goose, and it means no good, I'll be bound'; didn't I, Mrs. Upton?"

"You did, Mrs. Bellows," said Upton, "and I said to Mrs. Bellows, there's more in that than meets the eye, and I shouldn't be surprised if the poor dear Queen had some shocking accident or didn't live through the night, and someone ought to shoot that bird, flying about like that, and everyone said it was a shame and bound to bring bad luck, and so it was."

"And the soldiers were that military, miss," continued Mrs. Bellows, "and then there was the rain, and never in all my born days did I see so many umbrellows, quite a grove as you might say, and then the men came along to water the roads, though not necessary, as you well may say, miss, but orders is orders. And the sun come out, and the carriages come rolling through the gate, and the crowd began to squeege, and I wouldn't have missed it for five hundred pound."

"And Mrs. Bellows's nephew was very genteel, miss," said Upton, "and he saw two men with his own eyes that had their legs broke in the crowd, and a poor woman that had been kicked in the face by a horse. All knocked to a jelly before her eyes her face was, and they say she'll never look out of one eye again."

"And I lost my umbrellow coming back, and Mrs. Upton had her bonnet knocked right over her eyes," said Mrs. Bellows, "but here I stand gossiping when what you young ladies want is a nice cup of tea, and my girl gone trapesing out I'll be bound, and good gracious if there isn't my front door bell," upon which she left the room in great haste, followed by Upton.

The Coronation has indeed brought all classes together and at no other time could I have tolerated such conversation from Upton, who will doubtless need taking down after this.

The front door bell turned out to be Mr. Tom Ingoldsby, just back from the Abbey. He came to tell us that his family had decided to drive out and see the illuminations after dinner, and invited us to join them. We were not to make any change in our toilettes, and he offered to wait and escort us to Mivart's. Emily and I accepted with alacrity. I would have liked to have some news of my father and Ned, but knowing that they would probably be out till late, I contented myself with leaving a message with Mrs. Bellows to tell them where we had gone.

On our arrival at Mivart's we sat down to dinner in the Ingoldsbys' private room.

"Well, girls," said old Mr. Ingoldsby, "we had a rare time in the Abbey, I can tell you, and the fun of it is I saw some neighbours of ours in the country who had paid four times as much as we paid and weren't in half such good places. My Tom is a good hand at a bargain, and I don't regret the money I spent on our tickets."

"I have never got up so early in my life," said Mrs. Seaforth. "Only fancy, Emily, we were woken by the horrid cannon at four o'clock and we had to be in our places in the Abbey by six o'clock, or I am sure we never should have got in. But it all looked very fine, and after all one need never go to a coronation again."

"It was certainly a complete change," said Mr. Tom Ingoldsby, "from the venerable grey stone building to which we are accustomed. The monuments were all boarded over to preserve them from injury, galleries were erected everywhere and hung with rich draperies. The musicians were a fine sight in their gallery, which was draped with crimson and yellow. The choristers were, of course, in white, the canons in their black gowns and red hoods, while the orchestra were dressed in some kind of uniform richly trimmed with gold. Sir George Smart, their leader, seemed to have lent his name to the appearance of his helpers."

"Did you notice the Prussian Ambassador?" asked Mr. Seaforth. "When he arrived in his place he took one look at the musicians' gallery and actually screamed with delight. He must have wanted to scream to a different tune when the music began, for anything more execrable I have never heard."

"Come, come, Charles," said Mr. Tom, "you are unreasonable. Say that the oboes and bassoons were united in a sturdy English determination to play out of tune; say that Sir George Smart cannot conduct and play the organ simultaneously, except as a means of earning double fees; say that the Westminster boys gave the most inharmonious and murderous scream of greeting that ever was heard—but do not, Charles, oh do not say that the music was not in the best English tradition."

"It seemed very peculiar to me to hear people cheer in the Abbey," said Mrs. Seaforth. "I mean it did not give one the impression of an ordinary service, did it?"

"Well, my love, we may say that it was quite extraordinary," replied her husband, "and I must say the cheers for the Duke of Wellington were particularly gratifying to an old soldier like myself, though even they were nothing compared with the noise of the people and the instruments when the Queen at last came in from her tiring room."

"It made me proud to be an Englishman," said Mr. Ingoldsby. "Thady, look after the wine; the gentlemen aren't drinking. Come Caroline, you need to keep your strength up, you know. I must say I should have been glad of a drink in the Abbey, sitting there all those hours. I can't think how the Queen got through with it."

"Sure, your honour," said Thady, Mr. Seaforth's Irish servant, of whom I had before heard, "Her Majesty wasn't needing to be dry at all, at all. I got a peep into the chapel, King Edward's Chapel I think it is they call it, because being Protestants they don't call him a saint, bad cess to them! and there on the altar was a grand refreshment set out for Her Majesty, with custards and jellies and poultry and nuts and apples and wine and all. Sure, your honour needn't be unasy about the royal darling."

"That's enough, Thady," said Mr. Seaforth. "Put the wine on the table and you can go."

"Faith, I think the ould Lord that fell down on the steps in front of the Queen must have been at that same chapel," said Thady, quite unabashed by his master's rebuke. "It's myself would have rowled downstairs if I'd had a drop too much of the craythur and then to kneel on the steps in front of the whole world."

"Go downstairs, sir," said Charles Seaforth, and Thady vanished from the room.

"I apologize for my man," said Mr. Seaforth. "He is a good creature, but he drives me out of patience ten times a day."

As he said these words, Thady reappeared at the door, announcing "Mr. Darnley to see the company," and then departed once more, only pausing in the door to execute a few steps of an Irish jig. Mr. Darnley was cordially welcomed by the Ingoldsbys and placed himself at my side.

"I could not get away from the club earlier," he said. "We had about two thousand persons there, and six hundred ladies, and our French chef, Soyer, surpassed himself with the breakfast. I then went to Queen Street, but learning that Miss Harcourt and Miss Dacre had already left, I followed them here. I hope, Miss Harcourt, that your father will relent towards the Reform Club when he learns that they gave the largest patriotic breakfast of any club in London."

"I am sure," said I, "that your sentiments are truly loyal, Mr. Darnley. But as for my father and Ned, I am a little anxious. I know that gentlemen do not like to be asked to account for their actions, but it is not like my father to leave me for so long without news of him, and since what you told me about his playing high at White's," said I, lowering my voice, "a sentiment of anxiety has never been absent from my mind."

"If what I said has given any uneasiness to you, I wish I had never spoken," said Mr. Darnley gravely. "But you are tired by today's exertions and exaggerate your fears. If I can be of any assistance, I hope you will command me. I am certain to see Ned somewhere and will make inquiries from him."

I thanked him, and promised to banish from my mind as far as possible these foolish alarms. But what sense of security his promise of help imparted!

Mrs. Seaforth now pleaded fatigue, so she and her husband stayed in the hotel, while the rest of us, in Mr. Ingoldsby's carriage, went to see the illuminations. The carriage had to take its place in a long line which was slowly proceeding along the route taken earlier in the day by the Royal Procession. We could hardly proceed at more than a foot pace, and the police ordered the coachmen to keep to the right of the road. The illuminations were beyond my wildest dreams. All the clubs had vied with one another, and it was difficult to award the palm, though Crockford's, with the words VICTORIA REGINA in letters of fire six feet high, was among the finest. The Athenaeum had a large bulging British Crown all in gas, and the Ordnance Office was a blaze from top to bottom. We drove slowly along Cockspur Street and part way along the Strand, where we were particularly struck by the premises of the London Tea Company, who had a transparency tastefully outlined with coloured lamps and the words "Our Angel Queen, Huzza".

Returning past the National Gallery whose whole front was hung with lamps, we proceeded past Howell and James's brilliant gas illuminations in the Quadrant, up Regent Street, and so back to our lodgings.

I had very little to say during the drive, being, to tell the truth, excessively tired by the day's exertions and oppressed by a feeling of coming misfortune I could not explain. Emily, on the contrary, was in the highest spirits and laughed and talked with the two Mr. Ingoldsbys all the time. Mr. Darnley also said very little, though what he said was well chosen, and his presence was a solace to me.

Arrived at Queen Street I inquired whether my father or Ned had come in, and learning that neither had been heard of since the morning, my heart sank. Mr. Ingoldsby, with genuine kindness, pressed us to come to his hotel for the night, but I declined.

"Miss Harcourt," said Mr. Darnley, "I do beg you not to be alarmed. Your father has probably found old friends at his club, and as for Ned, you know what young men are. If it would be of any assistance to you, I will come here early tomorrow morning, to offer my services, though I am certain they will not be needed."

"Thank you very much indeed," said I. "You are kindness itself."

By this time my fears had communicated themselves to Emily. We sat up till late, listening to the cries from the street, and tormenting ourselves by trying to imagine what had occurred. Emily confessed to me that her seeming gaiety during the evening had merely masked an aching heart, and we mingled our tears. About four o'clock in the morning an unsteady step was heard on the stairs. Emily and I, who had fallen asleep in our chairs, sprang to our feet. It was Ned, looking as done up as he did after the rowing match.

"What have you been doing, Ned?" I asked, drawing aside the curtains and letting the morning light into the room.

"Been to the theatre," said Ned, rather thickly. "Been to *all* the theatres. All free tonight because of Coronation. Went to the lot of them and saw lots of good fellows. Saw the governor in queer company too. Governor says he'll cut his throat and blow his brains out, but that's all my eye. Give us soda-water, Fan, there's a good girl."

He leaned his head on his arms and at once went to sleep. Emily, with great spirit, shook him violently by the arm and poured some soda-water over his head, which revived him sufficiently to get upstairs, though incapable of speech. The reader may imagine in what agony of sleepless anxiety Emily and I passed the next few hours. The sunlight appeared a mockery, and when we did snatch a little sleep it was feverish and unrefreshing. At nine o'clock Upton brought a message that Mr. Darnley had called and sent his apologies for coming so early, but thought we might like to see him. Much comforted by this proof of reliability I finished dressing and went downstairs with Emily.

CHAPTER 10

MY HAPPIEST MOMENT

As soon as I got into the room, "I do hope," said I to Mr. Darnley, "that you will not think it wrong of me to receive you at this hour, but under the circumstances, and as Emily and I have not slept all night, and we are sure you bring news, you will be kind enough to excuse me."

At this incoherent speech Mr. Darnley pressed my hand kindly and replied, "I do bring news of your father, Miss Harcourt, who will shortly rejoin you, I trust. But I regret to say that I could hear nothing of Ned."

"He came back at four o'clock this morning, in a very intoxicated state," said I severely, "and is now asleep."

"He needs to sleep," said Emily tenderly, "after coming home so late. The poor fellow was so exhausted, Mr. Darnley, that he actually fell asleep before our eyes, and we were obliged to rouse him before we could get him to go to bed."

"In fact," said I, "Emily had to pour the soda-water on his head."

At this Mr. Darnley laughed outright, but Emily was displeased.

"I blame myself for having done it," said she. "He looked so pale and noble in his sleep, but we had to get him to go to bed somehow."

"But what of my father?" said I. "Pray tell us the worst, Mr. Darnley."

"I hope," answered Mr. Darnley, "that the worst may not be so very bad. I inquired at various clubs and gaming houses last night after I had left you, and heard on various hands that Mr. Harcourt—I cannot disguise it from you—had been playing very heavily and losing. About two o'clock I was fortunate enough to run into him in St. James's Street. He was in such a state of mind that I could not dare to let him out of my sight, and feeling that his appearance here at such an hour, and in such a condition, would terrify you and Miss Dacre even more than his unexplained absence, I took him to the Hummums in Covent Garden and engaged a room. I remained with him till he fell asleep and have left my man there with orders to bring him to you in my cab when he wakes. I then returned to my club, snatched an hour's sleep, and came to tell you the result of my efforts."

I was unable to speak. Shame at my father's conduct, apprehension for the future, gratitude to Mr. Darnley, all these roused in my bosom such conflicting emotions that speech was impossible.

"I hope," said Mr. Darnley, misinterpreting my silence, "that I have not presumed too far in my anxiety to be of use to Miss Harcourt."

"Indeed you have not," cried Emily, pushing in as usual. "You have acted most kindly and properly, but that is no more than one would expect. Fanny, is not Mr. Darnley the most thoughtful and generous of creatures?"

"He is, he is," I murmured faintly, and extended my hand in gratitude to Mr. Darnley. He raised it respectfully to his lips and saulted it, while a thrill ran through my whole being. We both remained mute, and might have so stayed for a long time, such was our mutual embarrassment, when a loud knocking was heard at the front door. Emily ran to the window.

"It is your cabriolet, Mr. Darnley," she cried. "That must be Mr. Harcourt returning."

My father's steps were heard on the stairs and he entered. I was so shocked by his appearance that I clung to Emily for support. He had evidently slept in his clothes, his linen was crumpled, his face unshaven, his hair in disorder, and he looked fully ten years older than when I had last seen him.

"Oh, Papa," I gasped, "where have you been? Emily and I have been frightened out of our senses. We sat up all night wondering what had become of you. How could you be so inconsiderate? We could not think what had happened."

"And now you know, I suppose, as I see Darnley is here before me," said my father. "You are a good fellow, Darnley, and these girls are fools. Sitting up all night! Sitting up never did any good unless there was something to sit up for. You can sit up for the rest of your life, Fan, for you soon won't have a bed to lie on. I have been an old fool and played too deep. How to tell your mother I don't know. Damned scoundrels saw I was a country pigeon and they plucked me clean. Bring me some soda-water, Fan."

I poured a glass from the remains of what Ned had had last night, sooner than bring the servants into the room.

"I had better leave you now, sir," said Mr. Darnley, "and if I can be of any assistance to you in any way, I beg that you will let me know. Do not think that I am presuming on our acquaintance if I suggest that a slight loan might be of use to you."

I had thought my father would have had one of his rages at such a suggestion, but he answered, "You are a Heart of Oak, Darnley, but I've enough to settle our bills and go home. It's the principal that's gone, my boy, not the petty cash. Don't go yet. Where's that scoundrel Ned?"

As he spoke my unlucky brother Ned made his appearance in a shawl dressing-gown and red morocco slippers. His hair also was ruffled and his cheek unshaven, and his face of surprise at seeing us all would have been comical had we had the spirits to laugh.

"Good lord, Governor," said Ned, "so you made a night of it

too! If you've got a head like mine, I'm confoundedly sorry for you."

"You'd better be sorry for yourself," said my father angrily.

"So I am," said Ned. "We made a real night of it, I and a dozen fellows. It was famous fun, I can tell you. We went to four theaters, they were free you know last night, and we walked down Regent Street arm in arm and the police couldn't stop us. As for the tapemen, the special policemen you know, they were all beastly intoxicated and lying about in the gutters in a very *special* fashion. Lord, it was famous! We smashed a lot of coloured lamps, and we went to the Cider Cellar and all got as drunk as lords, and when I got home the girls thought I was the devil! I thought so, too, last night, with infernal red-hot pincers at my head and molten lead in my gullet. Governor, you have all my sympathy. Pass us the soda-water. You look even worse than I do."

"Confound you, sir!" cried my father, hitting the table with such vehemence that a book fell on to the floor, "have you no respect for your father?"

"Not this morning, sir," answered Ned coolly, picking up the book. As he replaced it on the table, a paper fluttered from it.

"Here's one of Emily's billy doos," said Ned, carelessly perusing it. "Oh, ho," he cried, his expression changing, "it's not Em's, it's Fan's. Oh, you sly minx! Listen, Hal.

'Oh, turn away those fawn-like eyes, and close the jalousie!
Thou canst not know how deep thou wound'st the heart till
     now so free.
The VAVASOUR, who in the fight was first among the brave,
Is now in silken fetters bound, FRANCESCA's hapless slave.'"

My feelings may be better imagined than described. It was Mr. Vavasour's verses, which I had left in the book, hoping to make Emily jealous. How justly was I to be punished!

"Here, what's this?" asked my father. "Fanny getting poems

from Vavasour? Damn those women, you can't keep them from
it. Just the same in Norfolk, always some of the officers hanging
round the house. Well, Fan, you can whistle for him to come
back now. All the clubs will know this morning that old Harcourt is broke, and you won't see your beau again in a hurry."

"Papa!" I cried. "How can you speak like that? Mr. Vavasour is
the merest acquaintance, and indeed I cannot think how those
foolish verses came there."

"He writes you pretty warm stuff for an acquaintance," said
Ned, whom I could have killed on the spot.

"Mr. Darnley," cried I, distracted, "surely——"

"I beg that Miss Harcourt will not trouble to make an explanation," said Mr. Darnley rising. "I have no right to demand
one. I have been mistaken and I acknowledge my mistake. I had
thought—but no! Farewell, Ned. Miss Dacre, I shall hope to
see you when you are back at Tapton. Mr. Harcourt, do not
forget that I am at your service."

So saying he walked loftily from the room, leaving me a prey
to despair. I blamed myself bitterly for my lightheaded conduct.
In truth I had forgotten all about the lines, and now they had
turned and rent me. I began to sob, and Emily came to my
assistance with sal volatile.

"Go it, Fan," said that odious Ned. "You'll get a dozen more as
good as Vavasour. I hate those conceited snobs of Oxonians."

"You must call him out," said my father.

"Call him out?" cried Ned, stupefied, "why?"

"Damme, sir, do you want me to tell you, and before Miss
Dacre, to protect your sister's reputation?" asked my father, now
well in one of his rages. "If I were a younger man I'd do it myself.
Why, sir, the fellow Vavasour has——" but I cannot bring
myself to set down on paper what my father said. I hid my face
in Emily's bosom and sobbed convulsively.

"I say, governor, this is going a bit too far," protested Ned.
"Vavasour's a snob, and I don't like him, but hang it all he's a
gentleman, and what's more I owe him ten quid, so I can't very

well call him out, can I? If you'll lend me the money, sir, I might have a go at it."

Upon this my father burst into the most fearful imprecations saying that we were all ruined, that his estate would have to be sold, and that Ned need not look forward to inheriting an acre or a penny.

"Oh, come, I say, you can't expect us to swallow that," said Ned. But so violently did my father insist on his ruin, that we began to feel convinced of the truth of what he said.

"Well," said Ned, "that's a famous piece of bad luck. I hoped I was still drunk and imagining it all, but this is too much even for the rum punch we had last night. Poor Fan, you won't get married at all now. What about a wash and a shave, sir? We both need it."

"I'll see you d——d first," cried my father. "You insult a man when he's down, do you? You insult your sister, sir? By the Lord, sir, you won't get married either. You are a beggar, and a beggar's son."

On hearing this, Emily rose to her feet, looking, were her features better, almost sublime. With much dignity she walked to where Ned was sitting, the picture of astonishment and horror. Laying her hand upon his dressing-gown, she said, "You forget, Mr. Harcourt, that I have a large fortune of my own. That fortune is Ned's on the day that he marries me."

"Oh, I say, Em, you *are* a trump," cried Ned, rapturously kissing her hand. "We'll be as happy as badgers in a hole with your money. Look here, Em, when your father dies, not that I wish the old reverend any ill, but one must look ahead a bit you know, why shouldn't Hal give me the living? It's a good one, and I'll take orders as soon as I can, and we'll have a famous time and keep a pack of beagles and go to all the races. Hal has some good shooting at Tapton, I believe, and so have the Ingoldsbys at Tappington Everard."

Emily gazed proudly upon him, like a mother upon a favourite child. Happy Emily, who could offer her hand and fortune to the man of her heart, even if it were only Ned! I, alas, had not a penny to offer, and was for ever estranged from the best, the noblest of beings, and by my own fault. My father, who had been staring at this scene with lustreless eyes, now rose, and loudly d——ing his eyes and soul, left the room.

"My dearest Fanny, calm yourself," said Emily, "and do you, Ned, go and make yourself fit to be seen at once."

Ned shuffled away in his slippers and Emily spoke to me with such consoling kindness that my sobs redoubled.

"As for Mr. Vavasour's foolish verses," said she, "we will tear them up and forget them," upon which she reduced the card to the smallest fragments and threw them behind the grate.

A fresh peal at the front door bell presently made me jump from my seat in a transport of nerves, nor were my apprehensions unjustified, for it was Mr. Vavasour!

"Tell Mr. Harcourt and Mr. Ned," said Emily to Matthews, "that Mr. Vavasour is here, and beg them to come down the moment they are dressed."

Mr. Vavasour seemed strangely ill at ease. I had never before known him at a loss for conversation and did not feel inclined to help him. After much beating about the bush, he delivered to me a note from his aunt, which I asked permission to read at once.

"Oh, it is of no particular importance," said he nervously, "pray read it when I have gone. I only wished to have a word with you and then I will take my leave."

"Pardon me," said Emily, "I think Fanny had better read it now, in case there is any answer to be sent."

Encouraged by Emily's firmness I opened the note and read it, while she looked over my shoulder, an act which I was too much upset to resent as I would when myself. It was a cold and civil note, regretting that Mrs. Vavasour would be going out of town to her ward's country estate on the following day, and must therefore excuse herself from seeing us again before she left.

"My aunt hopes, I hope, we both hope, that you will understand, Miss Harcourt," said Mr. Vavasour, fidgeting with his chains.

"I understand perfectly," said I, fixing my glance upon him and feeling my courage return at this piece of impertinence, "and was about to write a similar note to Mrs. Vavasour myself, as I have persuaded my father to leave London and return to our *real* friends."

Mr. Vavasour looked foolish. "May I," said he, "beg a word with Miss Harcourt in private?"

"I think not," said I. "From Miss Dacre I have no secrets, nor have I from my father and brother," said I, as Papa and Ned, both very much improved in appearance, entered the room, followed by Ned's dog.

"Secrets? What's that?" asked my father.

For once my father's annoying curiosity had its uses.

"Oh, nothing, sir," said I, "only that Mr. Vavasour wished to speak with me in private. I cannot conceive any reason for such a request and must really beg to be excused. He brings me a note from Mrs. Vavasour, civilly declining the pleasure of our company for the future."

"Cross-eyed old bitch," said my father, almost pleasantly, so does shaving and a clean shirt refresh a man. "She liked the old Norfolk squire well enough when she thought he was a plum— set her cap at him, oh no! But now he is penniless he must eat the cold shoulder. Damme, hers would be a scraggy one!"

At this joke my father laughed quite in his old way.

"Miss Harcourt," said Mr. Vavasour earnestly, "you have a generous heart. May I presume upon its kindness to ask you to let me have back the book that I gave you? You will doubtless have no further use for it."

He said this with a meaning look, which, however, I did not choose to notice.

"I am sure Fan will give it back to you," said Ned, "provided she may keep the dedication. That was a famous piece of work."

"I suppose," said Emily, "you would like for 'Francesca' to put, 'Almeria.' 'Almeria's hapless slave' would not sound so badly."

At this Ned burst out laughing so loudly that Mr. Vavasour turned quite pale.

"Miss Harcourt, I trust in your discretion," he said, casting an appealing glance at me. "Permit me to take my leave."

"After him, old girl," cried Ned to the dog, who flew like an arrow after our departing guest. Emily and I sprang to the window and were in time to perceive the languid Oxonian actually running down Queen Street, with Ned's dog, the sweetest and mildest of creatures, snapping at his heels. Mr. Tom Ingoldsby, who was coming up the street, leant against the railings splitting his sides with laughter, tradesmen's boys hooted, maidservants jeered, pot-boys cried "Stop Thief!", other dogs joined in the chase, and so the romantic Vavasour vanished from our lives for ever.

"Lassy me!" said Emily, "it's Tom Ingoldsby. I declare I had forgotten that we were to go to the Hyde Park Fair with them. Shall we send him away, Mr. Harcourt?"

"No, no, my girl," said my father who was roaring with laughter, despite his dejection, at Mr. Vavasour's discomfiture. "You and Fan and Ned go and amuse yourselves."

"Look here, governor," said Ned, "I'll stay here. Can't desert a sinking ship you know. Tom will take the girls along."

My father was so much affected that he turned away. Ned whispered to me to keep my spirits up, and that it would be much better for me to show myself as if nothing had happened. So, though with a heavy heart, I put on my walking dress and went with Emily and Mr. Tom to Mivart's.

Old Mr. Ingoldsby received us with particular kindness and asked meaningly what was the news with us.

"None, sir," said I, "except that Emily has consented to become a sister to me. She and Ned are to be married when old Mr. Dacre is no more. She is a lucky creature," I added, my eyes filling with tears.

"Tut, tut, Miss Harcourt," said old Mr. Ingoldsby, "don't cry. A little bird tells me that you will be down in our part of the country before long, and you will find a hearty welcome from all of us at Tappington Everard. Cheer up, for we must smoke Emily about this affair."

A great deal of congratulating and joking then took place. Mr. Ingoldsby insisted that we should have some lunch before starting on our expedition, and ordered champagne to drink Emily's and Ned's health. In the general gaiety I almost forgot my own troubles. Mr. Tom rallied Emily archly about the fatal letter T.

"My heart is broken now that you prefer N.," said he. "And what will poor Hal Darnley do?"

Emily said something in a low voice to him which I could not hear. I felt so wretchedly uncomfortable I could have cried, and was glad when we were *en route* for Hyde Park. Mr. Tom excused himself saying that he had an important engagement, but the rest of us, including Mrs. Seaforth, who insists upon exposing herself to every kind of fatigue in almost a *bold* way, considering her condition, set out on foot.

Never have I seen such a sight. Several acres of the park must have been covered with the booths, tents, and sideshows there erected. Here one might see a Punch and Judy show, there a tent for beer or refreshments. Loud-voiced men called our attention by shouting the wares they had to sell, or extolling the rarities they had to show. Ruffianly looking fellows, like Bill Sikes, jostled and hustled the crowd while their light-fingered associates, Artful Dodgers in the fullest sense of the words, took advantage of the confusion to make off with handkerchiefs, reticules, watch-chains, and other small articles. Warned by Mr. Seaforth we avoided the thickest parts of the crowd and were lucky enough to escape the attentions of the pickpockets.

Others were not so fortunate, and we saw a stout, elderly woman of respectable appearance run up to a policeman, saying she had been robbed of a silk handkerchief. The policeman very

civilly asked her to describe the individual who had taken it, but
she could only say that she had been jostled in the crowd and
found her handkerchief gone. Just at that moment another
policeman came up, with a thin ratfaced man in custody.

"Here's another of the watch-and-chain gang, Wickens,"
said he to the first policeman. "I nabbed him with these 'ere
watches and five silk hankerchers, just as he was a-trying to
pinch an old gent's pocket book."

"Let's see the wipes," said the first officer.

Accordingly the second man exhibited a number of silk
handkerchiefs, one of which the woman asserted with loud
outcries to be hers.

"Well, you'll have to come along to the station and tell the
Inspector there about it, mum," said the second man.

"But it's my hankercher," cried the stout woman. "Any one as
knows me will tell you so. I live down near the New Cut, and if
that partickler hankercher ain't mine, you ask all the neighbours
or ask my little girl here."

"Afraid we haven't time to go to the New Cut, mum," said the
officer called Wickens, grinning, "but we'll hear what the little
gel's got to say."

"Speak up, lovey," said the woman, "and tell the gentleman
about auntie's hankercher."

"Please sir," piped up the little girl, holding up a large ban-
danna, "here's auntie's wipe. She told me to prig it off an old
party, and I done it that quiet as he never seed me."

At this the stout woman flew at the little girl and began
cuffing her. The child screamed, and the policemen took them
both away, kicking and scratching, to the police station.

"It is unfortunate," said Mr. Seaforth, "that we missed the
balloon ascent yesterday, which must have been very impressive."

"But, Charles dear, they came down in Marylebone Lane, you
told me so yourself," said Mrs. Seaforth, "and I cannot think

that it is worth going up in a balloon to get to Marylebone, whatever people may say about science."

"Come along, girls, and see the donkey races," called old Mr. Ingoldsby.

A number of sailors added here to the gaiety of the scene, as these gallant fellows are always in the best of spirits. A band of them were patronizing the donkey races, and we were amused to see one who had been unhorsed, or rather unassed, run forward, and seizing the foremost donkey by the tail endeavour to keep it back while he caught his own steed. Mr. Seaforth remarked that the race was hardly being run under Jockey Club rules.

Another party of gallant tars was gathered round the so-called aerial ships, and was expressing in no measured terms its contempt for such land-lubberly affairs. A dispute had arisen between two of the proprietors and a party of the sailors, and a policeman coming up inquired "what the row was about."

"Why," said one of the sailors, "this here feller calls his —— bumboat a ship, and so, d'ye see, he was on the gangway and I gave him a shove, quite a gentle hit-like, and down he goes, plumpendickler on the ground, starn uppermost."

"Vy," screamed the gentleman in question, "if you ain't the werry cove as cotched me a preshus whop under my ear, wot knocked me bang out!"

"And you're the werry identical vun," cried his friend, "as giv'd me sich a gallus kick as I ain't bin able to sit down comfortable ever since."

The policeman recommended them all to be on their good behaviour and walked away, saying he would keep an eye on them. The owners of the aerial ship went grumbling back to their employ, while the sailors, seizing a number of not unwilling females who were standing invitingly by, drew them to a booth where all were soon engaged in the mazy convolutions of the dance.

We strolled about for some time, noticing among other evidences of the care of our police force that there was a marquee for the reception of lost children, which is indeed a tribute to the humanity of our times. But the noise was excessive and the dust made the atmosphere as thick as though there were a fog, so we were quite glad, after purchasing a printed souvenir of the Fair, to take a coach back to Mivat's. Old Mr. Ingoldsby pressed us warmly to stay and dine, but we were both so tired after our sleepless night, and I for one so oppressed with anxiety, that we excused ourselves. We therefore made our farewell to the Ingoldsby family, who were to return to the country on the following day, Emily charging them with affectionate messages for her father.

Old Mr. Ingoldsby was particularly affectionate to me, patting my hand with various sly looks, which were at the time totally incomprehensible to me, while the Seaforths in the kindest manner expressed the pleasure they would have in seeing me in their part of the country.

"I fear," said I, "that I am not likely to be in Kent. My father has to return to Norfolk at once on business, and unless he will permit me to visit Emily, it is not likely that I shall be able to leave home for some time to come."

"Stranger things have happened," said Mrs. Seaforth, "and I count upon seeing you before long. In fact, I have hopes that you may be a godmother to the next little Seaforth. The sixth letter of the alphabet is a favourite in our neighbourhood, you know," she added archly.

This reminder of what I had lost filled me with such misery and confusion that I could barely stammer my thanks and escape.

"Dearest Fanny, pray do not take on so," said Emily as we walked back to Queen Street. "Darnley cannot be indifferent to you. Indeed his annoyance over the verses proves as much. Patience, my love, and all will be well."

"It is all very well for you to say so, Emily," I replied, "who can marry Ned when you please. But my position is indeed unfortunate. If Papa's affairs are so bad, we shall have to live in quite a humble way, I suppose, and never leave Norfolk, so what chance shall I have of seeing him again? Besides, my shocking levity has exposed me to his righteous censure, and no explanation can efface the impression this morning must have made on his mind. Oh, Emily, I am so very unhappy."

Emily did not attempt to console me, and we arrived at Queen Street in silence. In the sitting-room we found Ned and Mr. Tom Ingoldsby.

"Where is Papa?" I asked, almost afraid to hear that his lifeless corpse, dripping with river weeds, or gore-bespattered, lay in the back bedroom.

"Out with Hal," said Ned. "I say, Fan, Hal is a famous good fellow. He has been with the governor all afternoon, he and Tom here, going into his affairs, and he has taken him off to see his lawyer."

Noble, noblest Darnley!

"And is Mr. Harcourt really ruined?" asked Emily, with what was, I think, not so much want of tact as a sincere wish to find Ned penniless and totally dependent on her.

"It is difficult to say how he stands," said Mr. Tom, "but it might be worse. It looks as though he would have to sell his estate, and if he does he will be in a position to pay off his debts and have a small income."

"It's a cursed shame for my mother and you, Fan," said Ned with a wry face. "William and I can make our own way, and when my mother dies you know we inherit a small sum from her settlement; and that the governor luckily can't touch. Look here, Fan, when Em and I are married you can come and stay with us at the Rectory, but I'll have to take orders first, of course, and then we must wait for Em's father—ahem."

"Thank you, Ned," I said, "But you are speaking as if you were certain of having Tapton Rectory."

"So I am," said Ned. "Hal has promised it. He's a famous fellow."

Emily expressed her satisfaction, and I tried to show the

pleasure that I truly felt, but how difficult is it to join in the rejoicing of others when one's soul is steeped in misery and despair. Another proof of Darnley's noble and disinterested conduct, and my fatal loss!

As Emily and Ned were now carrying on that kind of amorous bickering which is so very uninteresting to all save the parties concerned, Mr. Tom Ingoldsby drew me to the window.

"Dear Miss Harcourt," said he, "I am not an old man, but I am a good deal older than you, and I am going to take advantage of this position to speak as a friend, or an elder brother with rather more experience than Ned."

"You are very kind," said I, not taking much notice.

"Ned is right about your father's affairs," he continued. "I was with Darnley and your father this afternoon, and it is true that he will be a poor man when his debts are paid. He has acted very wrongly, almost criminally, but it is not for me to judge him. You ought, however, to know two things. It is Darnley who will purchase your father's estate. This is not to be generally known, for Hal is the last man in the world to make his good deeds public. The world will only know that a buyer has been found. Darnley will put a steward in to manage the estate and ask your father to live in his own house as a tenant if he so wishes. If Ned cares to buy it back later with his wife's money, he can do so. If not, Hal will probably leave it to one of his children."

"Is he then to marry?" I faltered.

"That I am not at liberty to say," replied Mr. Tom. "The other thing which I think you should know is that Darnley is presenting the living of Tapton not so much to Miss Dacre's husband as to Miss Harcourt's brother."

My head was in a whirl. Darnley, whom I had treated so ill, the benefactor of our family! Darnley presenting a living, of whose reversion he might have disposed for a large sum, to Ned, because he was my brother! Such nobility, such generosity filled my heart so full that I had to turn my face away to hide the tears that trickled down my cheek.

"Poor little Fanny," said Mr. Tom, putting his arm round me in such a kind and brotherly way that I felt no resentment, "dry your eyes and be a good girl."

His droll way of speaking made me laugh and I was soon able to converse with the others. My father shortly returned. He refused to discuss business till he had dined, and Mr. Tom obligingly stayed to dinner, where by his jokes and puns he kept my father's spirits from being too low. After dinner we gathered in the sitting-room, and my father, with real remorse, told us the position of his affairs, which was much as we had heard already.

"Darnley has been a good friend to me," he said. "He may be a Radical, but if all Radicals were like him I would shake hands even with Hume. His lawyer is going to see to the selling of the place, and I may be able to stay on as tenant, if I can bear it without the horses and dogs. It would break your poor mother's heart to go, Fan, else I'd go and live in a cottage somewhere. By God, to live in my own house as another man's guest will be the worst of my punishment. There's no fool like an old fool. And I've some bad news for you, Fan."

"What," cried I, "nothing, I hope, has happened to Mr. Darnley?"

"Darnley?" said my father. "Not that I know of, unless he has met with an accident since I left him an hour ago, and I hope he hasn't, as he is to come here at nine o'clock with some papers. No, no, my poor girl, it's about some one quite different."

Our curiosity was roused, and we begged to know what this mysterious piece of news might be.

"Darnley's lawyer told us," said my father, avoiding my glance, "that he had today received instructions to prepare marriage settlements for that damned Frenchified Vavasour, and Lady Almeria What's-her-name, and they are to be married as soon as possible."

"Sooner he than I," said Mr. Tom. "From what I have seen and heard of her ladyship, she will wear the breeches, and lead him a pretty dance into the bargain."

"I hope she'll comb his hair with a three-legged stool," cried Ned, in one of his vulgar phrases.

"And he will have to know that shocking Mrs. Norton," said Emily.

"I think it an excessively good match," said I coldly. "Where there is a complete absence of heart on both sides, and an equality of fortune, we may expect the kind of marriage which the world calls happy."

"Good girl!" cried my father, "there's a spirit! I thought a girl of mine couldn't care for such a sneaking puppy, and I told Darnley so. Depend upon it, Darnley, I said, she'd got her head stuffed with some romantic nonsense because the fellow has greasy curls and a fine waistcoat. Depend upon it, I said, her heart's in the right place if she's her old father's daughter, as her mother says she is."

I threw up my eyes to heaven at my father's coarseness, but no one noticed me, as Matthews at this moment came into the room to say that one of the grooms from home was waiting below with an urgent letter for my father. A presentiment of evil seemed to strike us all. The man was shown up—it was the same groom who had ridden for the doctor when my mother was taken ill—and touched his hat to my father, who rose to take the letter.

"Read it, Ned," said my father, sitting down again heavily. "By God, I've had all I can stand today."

The letter was from our family physician to tell my father that my mother had been taken suddenly and violently worse, and that her recovery was impossible. While urging my father to return at once, he did not disguise his fear that my mother would probably have ceased to breathe. Ned handed the letter to my father, who sat as one stunned. At last he said, "Thank God the poor creature won't know that I have ruined her children. Come down, Ned, and get this fellow to tell me what he can. Fan, you had better pack your things. We must go tomorrow morning."

He and Ned, followed by the groom, then went downstairs, leaving me with Emily and Mr. Tom.

"Let me express my sympathy," said Mr. Tom in his kindest manner, "and my hopes that Mrs. Harcourt may be spared to see you before the end. Emily, if you can pack your things in time, you had better come back with us tomorrow; there is a seat in the carriage. For tonight, Miss Harcourt will be glad of your company and sisterly affection."

"I will pack now," said Emily, "if you will stay with Fanny, and I will also tell Fanny's maid to see to her things, and explain the situation to Mrs. Bellows."

So saying, she embraced me warmly and departed.

"Please, Mr. Ingoldsby, do not talk to me," said I.

"Indeed I won't, child," said kind Mr. Tom. He sat by me at the window, holding my hand, while I endeavoured to collect myself; but it was in vain; tears poured from my eyes.

"That's right, poor little Fanny," said he in his droll way, "a good cry is the best medicine, and then you will feel much better."

With true delicacy he looked out of the window while still holding my hand, so that I could cry undisturbed. Presently I heard a ring at the bell and people talking at the door. A voice that I knew only too well was telling Matthews to give a packet of papers to Mr. Harcourt, and Matthews was telling him the sad news from home.

"Excuse me for a moment," said Mr. Tom, and letting go my hand he darted from the room and downstairs. I was too weak with unhappiness to take much notice, or care what happened, and when I heard the front door shut, I could not cry any more bitterly than I had been doing. The drawing-room door re-opened, footsteps crossed the floor, my hand was again held. A manly voice, thrilling with emotion, the voice I most loved and worshipped in the whole world, said in my ear, "The Zegri Ladye weeps."

"Mr. Darnley!" I faltered, rising to my feet. "Oh, can you forgive me?"

"Nay, it is you that must forgive me, my Fanny," said he drawing me to his bosom. "I was hasty. But let us forget all that is past. Mine be it hence forward to console and support my Zegri Ladye."

Our lips met. My senses swooned.

When the first transports were over, "We must not forget that good fellow Tom Ingoldsby," said *my* Darnley, for so I now could call him, "who is waiting outside to hear the news. Had it not been for his kindness I should have gone away without seeing you again."

Together—oh, rapturous word!—together we looked from the window. Mr. Tom was leaning against the railings on the opposite side of the road, conversing with a potboy from whom he had obtained a mug of beer.

"Tom, my dear fellow," cried Darnley, "you are a trump, and I am the happiest of men."

"Dear little Fanny," said Mr. Tom, coming below the window and raising his hat to me, "are you good and happy now?"

"I am, I am indeed," I said earnestly.

"Then," said Mr. Tom, "I shall go to bed. Good-night, and waving his hat he walked up Queen Street and disappeared round the corner.

POSTSCRIPT

*T*here is little to add to my narrative. My poor mother had breathed her last before we could reach her side, and was sincerely mourned, if not deeply regretted. Owing to my unprotected condition I persuaded my father to allow my marriage to Mr. Darnley to take place a month after her death. My little Victoria was born on the anniversary of her namesake's coronation. My father, as I think I mentioned before, has a competence sufficient to maintain him, but I have not seen him since my marriage.

I am the happiest of wives and mothers, and have no secrets from Mr. Darnley save those which expediency dictates. There was a great to-do about the missing copy of the *Ingoldsby Legends*, but as Mr. Darnley is an excellent customer, the bookseller agreed that the mistake must be his and sent another copy, whereupon I gave the unfortunate original to Emily. The Ingoldsby family flourish and Mr. Tom is in a way to become quite famous with his book. Should my expected child be a boy we intend to call him Thomas in gratitude to him. I hear that our Queen is also about to become a mother, but her child, though swathed in purple, can be no dearer to her than our offspring are to us. Emily says she cannot conceive why I spend so much time in the nursery.

"It is quite proper, my love," said I, when she had made this remark more often than I could bear, "that you should not yet know the joys of motherhood. Wait till you and Ned have been married for a year."

"A year!" cried Emily. "Lassy me, I hope I shan't wait as long as that."

I sometimes wonder how I ever came to make a friend of Emily.

APPENDIX
WITH NOTES

OCH! the Coronation! what celebration
  For emulation can with it compare?
When to Westminster the Royal Spinster,
  And the [1] Duke of Leinster, all in order did repair!
'Twas there you'd see the New Polishemen
  Making a skrimmage at half after four,
And the Lords and Ladies, and the Miss O'Gradys
  All standing round before the Abbey door.

Their pillows scorning, that self-same morning
  Themselves adorning, all by the candle light,
With roses and lilies, and daffy-down-dillies,
  And gould, and jewels, and rich di'monds bright.
And then approaches five hundred coaches,
  With [2] Giniral Dullbeak. — Och! 'twas mighty fine
To see how asy bould [3] Corporal Casey,
  With his swoord drawn, prancing, made them kape the line.

Then the Guns' alarums, and the [4] King of Arums,
  All in his Garters and his Clarence shoes,
Opening the massy doors to the bould Ambassydors,
  The [5] Prince of Potboys, and great haythen Jews;
'Twould have made you crazy to see [6] Esterhazy
  All jew'ls from jasey to his di'mond boots,
With [7] Alderman Harmer, and that swate charmer,
  The famale heiress, Miss Anjā-ly Coutts.

And Wellington walking with his swoord drawn, talking
  To [8] Hill and [9] Hardinge, haroes of great fame;
And [10] Sir De Lacy, and the [11] Duke Dalmasey,
  (They call'd him Sowlt afore he changed his name,)
Themselves presading [12] Lord Melbourne, lading
  The Queen, the darling, to her Royal chair,

And that fine ould fellow, the [13]Duke of Pell-Mello,
  The Queen of Portingal's Chargy-de-fair.

Then the Noble Prussians, likewise the Russians,
  In fine laced jackets with their goulden cuffs,
And the Bavarians, and the proud Hungarians,
  And Everythingarians all in furs and muffs.
Then [14]Misthur Spaker, with [15]Misthur Pays the Quaker,
  All in the Gallery you might persave,
But [16]Lord Brougham was missing, and gone a fishing,
  Ounly crass [17]Lord Essex would not give him lave.

There was [18]Baron Alten himself exalting,
  And [19]Prince Von Swartzenberg, and many more,
Och! I'd be bother'd, and entirely smother'd
  To tell the half of 'em was to the fore;
With the swate Peeresses, in their crowns and dresses,
  And Aldermanesses, and the Boord of Works;
But [20]Mehemet Ali said, quite gintaly,
  "I'd be proud to see the likes among the Turks!"

Then the Queen, Heaven bless her! och! they did dress her
  In her purple garaments, and her goulden Crown;
Like Venus or Hebe, or the Queen of Sheby,
  With eight young Ladies houlding up her gown.
Sure 'twas grand to see her, also for to he-ar
  The big drums bating, and the trumpets blow,
And [21]Sir George Smart! Oh! he play'd a Consarto,
  With his four-and-twenty fiddlers all on a row!

Then the [22]Lord Archbishop held a goulden dish up,
  For to resave her bounty and great wealth,
Saying "Plase your Glory, great Queen Vict-ory!
  Ye'll give the Clargy lave to dhrink your health!"
Then his Riverence, retrating, discoorsed the mating,
  "Boys! Here's your Queen! deny it if you can!
And if any bould traitour, or infarior craythur,
  Sneezes at that, I'd like to see the man!"

Then the Nobles kneeling to the Pow'rs appealing,
    "Heaven send your Majesty a glorious reign!"
And [23]Sir Claudius Hunter he did confront her,
    All in his scarlet gown and goulden chain.
The great [24]Lord May'r, too, sat in his chair too,
    But mighty sarious, looking fit to cry,
For the [25]Earl of Surrey, all in his hurry
    Throwing the thirteens, hit him in his eye.

Then there was preaching, and good store of speeching,
    With Dukes and Marquises on bended knee;
And they did splash her with raal Macasshur,
    And the Queen said, "Ah! then, thank ye all for me!"—
Then the trumpets braying, and the organ playing,
    And sweet trombones with their silver tones,
But [26]Lord Rolle was rolling;—'twas mighty consoling
    To think his Lordship did not break his bones.

Then the crames and the custards, and the beef and mustard,
    All on the tombstones like a poultherer's shop,
With lobsters and white-bait, and other swate-meats,
    And wine, and nagus, and Imparial Pop!
There was cakes and apples in all the Chapels,
    With fine polonies, and rich mellow pears,
Och! the [27]Count Von Strogonoff, sure he got prog enough,
    The sly ould Divil, underneath the stairs.

Then the [28]cannons thunder'd, and the people wonder'd,
    Crying, "God save Victoria, our Royal Queen!"
Och! if myself should live to be a hundred,
    Sure it's the proudest day that I'll have seen!
And now I've ended, what I pretended,
    This narration splendid in swate poe-thry,
Ye dear bewitcher, just hand the pitcher,
    Faith, it's meself that's getting mighty dhry!

Notes on Mr. Barney Maguire's Account of the Coronation

1. *The Duke of Leinster.* High Constable of Ireland.

2. *Giniral Dullbeak.* Sir James Charles Dalbiac, K.C.H.* But Mr. Maguire's name is an inspiration.

3. *Corporal Casey.* This hero was doubtless present, *teste* his countryman, but is among the number unrecorded.

4. *The King of Arums.* Sir William Woods, Deputy Garter, Clarenceux King of Arms, K.H.

5. *The Prince of Potboys.* Prince de Putbus, Ambassador Extraordinary from the King of Prussia.

6. *Esterhazy.* The resident Austrian Ambassador, Prince Esterhazy, G.C.B.

7. *Alderman Harmer.* Owner of the Radical *Weekly Despatch.* He began life as a weaver, then became a solicitor, and on becoming an Alderman in 1833 gave up his large practice, said to be worth £4,000 a year. He stood for Lord Mayor, but was defeated, partly owing to the venomous opposition of *The Times,* 1840.

8. *Hill.* Lord Hill, later Viscount Hill, G.C.B., &c. Distinguished in Egypt, Peninsular War, Waterloo. He was among the few cheered in the Abbey.

9. *Hardinge.* Sir Henry Hardinge, K.C.B., later Viscount Hardinge. He had been in the Peninsular War and at Quatre Bras.

10. *Sir De Lacy.* Sir George De Lacy Evans, K.C.B. India, Peninsular War, America, Waterloo. Commanded British Legion assisting Queen Christina against Don Carlos 1835–7. M.P. for Westminster. Greville says his new K.C.B.(1837) was much criticized in the clubs.

*Royal Hanoverian Guelphic Order, instituted by the Prince Regent in 1815. It was not conferred after the separation of the crowns of England and Hanover.

11. *The Duke Dalmasey.* Marshal Soult, Duke of Dalmatia, Ambassador Extraordinary from the King of the French. He was one of the most popular figures of the Coronation.

12. *Lord Melbourne.* Bore the sword of State in the Abbey.

13. *Duke of Pell-Mello.* Duke of Palmella, Ambassador Extraordinary from the Queen of Portugal. He was a familiar figure in London society, and must have held much the same place as the Marquis de Soveral later. He appears in Harriette Wilson's memoirs as one of the protectors of her sister Amy.

14. *Misthur Spaker.* James Abercromby, Speaker 1835–9.

15. *Misthur Pays the Quaker.* Joseph Pease, railway promoter. He was the first Quaker M. P., being allowed to take the oath by affiriming, 1833.

16. *Lord Brougham.* Essex and Brougham had been on good terms, but after the Reform Bill, Essex took Grey's side. At about this period Brougham went down to Cashiobury, Lord Essex's seat, uninvited, and was severely rebuffed, Lord Essex refusing to see him.

17. *Crass Lord Essex.* The fifth Earl married the singer, Miss Stephen, that year. She was present in the Abbey.

18. *Baron von Alten.* Count Alten, G.C.B., Ambassador Extraordinary from the King of Hanover.

19. *Prince von Swartzenberg.* Prince Schwartzenberg, Ambassador Extraordinary from the Emperor of Austria.

20. *Mehemet Ali.* All our researches fail to detect the presence of this person at the Coronation. Is it possible that Mr. Maguire confused him with Sarim Effendi, the Turkish Ambassador? We learn that on entering the Abbey Sarim Effendi "seemed absolutely bewildered, he stopped in astonishment and for some time could not be moved to his allotted place."

21. *Sir George Smart.* Musician and orchestral conductor, who produced Mendelssohn's *St. Paul* at Liverpool in 1836 and conducted most of the provincial festivals. Composer to the Chapel Royal. Conductor for funeral of George IV and Coronation of William IV and Queen Victoria.

22. *The Lord Archbishop.* The Archbishop of Canterbury, William Howley, D.D. The "Bounty and great wealth" were the offerings of first an ingot of gold of one pound's weight, and secondly a purse of gold. The Archbishop's words, slightly exaggerated by the enthusiastic Mr. Maguire, were: "Sirs, I here present unto you QUEEN VICTORIA, the undoubted QUEEN of this realm; wherefore, all you who are come this day to do your Homage, Are you willing to do the same?"

Greville describes him as "meek and quiet, not dignified, but very civil and attentive."

23. *Sir Claudius Hunter.* Lord Mayor, 1811–12.

24. *The Great Lord May'r.* Sir John Cowan, Bt.

25. *The Earl of Surrey.* Treasurer of the Household and heir of the Duke of Norfolk. After the homage he "threw the Coronation Medals about the choir and lower galleries," though we cannot discover that the Lord Mayor was hit in the eye. A "thirteen" was the Irish name for a silver shilling, worth thirteen pence at that time in the Irish coinage.

26. *Lord Rolle.* "This aged and infirm peer, upwards of 80 years old, stumbled and fell in ascending the steps to do his homage, when the Queen rose from her seat, extended her hand for him to kiss, and expressed a hope that his lordship was not hurt. This act of royal and gracious kindliness was instantly felt and appreciated by all the spectators who loudly and zealously applauded it."

27. *Count Von Strogonoff.* The Count Stroganov, Ambassador Extraordinary from the Emperor of Russia. There is no confirmation of Mr. Maguire's indictment, but a description of the lunch laid out on the altar in King Edward's chapel may be read in the journals of Queen Victoria, who was rather scandalized by it.

28. *The cannons thundered.* "A telegraphic communication was made from the floor through the roof (of the Abbey), and as the crown was placed on her head a rocket was fired and cannon thundered from the Park and Tower."